"All right," Annie agreed, not embarrassed at her husky whisper, "round one goes to you."

Luke smiled. "Not yet."

Her heartbeat raced. Luke shifted so that one of his thighs was over hers, pressing against her intimately. She knew she should want to stop the burn that was slowly building inside her, but she lay there—on her aunt's couch, at her aunt's ranch—holding her breath until it came out in a warm shuddering rush across his chin.

The midnight Texas air was melting-hot and sticky, but Annie didn't care. She wanted to take more of his weight. She wanted to rip off his shirt and feel his bare chest against her exposed breasts.

"I've wanted to kiss you since last night," he murmured, pressing his lips to her jaw.

"We just met last night."

"I know. Isn't it great?"

Annie smiled.

It sure was.

Dear Reader,

I'd been thinking about Luke for a long time before I actually wrote this book. I mean the man has been in my head for several years. Even the title came easily. The difficulty was finding the perfect woman for him. I have to admit that I went through several heroines in my mind and on paper. They were all too ordinary or not spunky enough. Finally, something my editor said to me brought Annie to life. I knew she was the one for Luke the first time she spoke.

I love that part about writing. When the story suddenly becomes so vivid in my head, it seems like magic. But then I have to write it. No magic there. Discipline and hard work get the pages done. And I love every minute of it.

Happy reading!

Debbi Rawlins

SLOW HAND LUKE
Debbi Rawlins

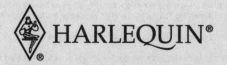

HARLEQUIN®

TORONTO • NEW YORK • LONDON
AMSTERDAM • PARIS • SYDNEY • HAMBURG
STOCKHOLM • ATHENS • TOKYO • MILAN • MADRID
PRAGUE • WARSAW • BUDAPEST • AUCKLAND

ISBN-13: 978-0-373-79316-7
ISBN-10:   0-373-79316-2

SLOW HAND LUKE

This edition published by arrangement with Harlequin Books S.A.

® and TM are trademarks of the publisher. Trademarks indicated with
® are registered in the United States Patent and Trademark Office, the
Canadian Trade Marks Office and in other countries.

www.eHarlequin.com

Printed in U.S.A.

ABOUT THE AUTHOR

Debbi Rawlins lives in central Utah—out in the country, surrounded by woods and deer and wild turkeys. It's quite a change for a city girl who didn't even know where the state of Utah was until four years ago. Of course, unfamiliarity never stopped her. Between her junior and senior years of college she spontaneously left home in Hawaii, and bummed around Europe for five weeks by herself. And much to her parents' delight, returned home with only a quarter in her wallet.

Books by Debbi Rawlins

HARLEQUIN BLAZE

*Men To Do
†Do Not Disturb

1

ANOTHER SUNNY SPRING day in Brooklyn. The punks would be out in full force. Annie Corrigan sighed as she stared out the small square window from the office she shared with three other cops. One more report to write and then she'd be out there, arguing with her partner over their cruiser's temperature controls.

Her phone rang and she had to stifle a yawn before answering. "Sergeant Corrigan."

"Hey, baby, it's me."

She closed her eyes, her chest tightening. "What do you want?"

"Is that any way to speak to—"

"Don't tell me." Her voice started to rise and she quickly lowered it. "You've been arrested again."

"Look, Annie, I was going to call you last week, maybe buy you some dinner, but I got busy. You know how it is."

Nothing changed. Nothing ever changed. Did he really expect her to believe more of his lies? "I told you not to call me at work."

"See, the thing is, baby, I did get in a small scrape. But I swear to you, this time it wasn't my fault."

She shook her head. It never was. "I have to go."

"Come on, baby, you aren't going to leave me locked up for the weekend."

"See you around, Pop," she said, and hung up.

She stared at the phone for a long time, anger and resentment burning in her gut. The guilt that crept in made her even angrier and she had to force herself to breathe. How many times had she bailed him out? Used her hard-earned money or called in one too many favors? When had he ever been there for her? All he'd done was lie. About Annie's mother. About everything.

"Monday's the deadline and you haven't done squat." Lisa dragged a chair closer to Annie's cluttered gray metal desk and adjusted her holster and gun before planting herself in Annie's face. "What's up with that?"

"Not now, okay?"

Lisa's blue eyes clouded with concern. "What's wrong?"

Annie started to shake her head although she knew better. She knew Lisa—her best friend, the sister she never had and an incredibly pushy broad. "It was Larry."

"In jail again?"

"Yep."

"Forget him."

Annie sighed. "Yep."

"Don't you dare feel guilty."

"Me? Hell, no. I'm not the parent. He's the one who screwed up." Except she did feel guilty, because she hated and loved him at the same time. Especially hated him for her longing for family and love that she couldn't quite shake. "Let's talk about something else."

Lisa hesitated, obviously wanting to belabor the moot point, however her face brightened. "Like the detectives exam?"

Annie stared at her friend. Another annoying issue. "I haven't decided to take it yet."

"Why not? You'd ace it."

"It's the cool uniform. I don't want to give it up."

Lisa laughed. "Yeah, guys think we're hot."

Annie smiled wryly. Guys either really got off on the whole uniform thing, or they ran the other way. Not much happened in between. Which left Annie with going to the movies on Friday nights with Lisa and playing softball with the whole gang at the neighborhood park on Saturday mornings.

"I like where I am." Comfortable. Familiar. Safe. Everything Annie wanted in life. "What's the big deal, anyway?"

"Ah, gee, let me think about it. Hmm, what sounds better…Sergeant Corrigan…Detective Corrigan? Not to mention a huge pay raise." She gave Annie a flat look and then her trademark nasal, "Hel-lo." Loud enough that the few officers still hanging around the precinct turned to look at them.

"Why aren't *you* taking the exam?" Annie asked.

"And embarrass my father? I barely made sergeant. I couldn't even pass *that* the first time."

Old argument. Useless to say anything. Annie had never figured out Lisa's lack of confidence. Sure, her dad was a decorated police captain, but he and Mrs. O'Brien were encouraging and understanding, the kind of great parents every kid dreamed of. Annie knew firsthand, since she'd lived with them for half her teen years.

Of course, Great Aunt Marjorie had always been there for Annie, a shoulder to lean on, someone who always listened without judgment—mostly from long distance. She lived on a small ranch in Texas where Annie had spent a few summers when she was little.

"Seriously, Annie, you'd be crazy not to go for it. Sanders and Jankowski are both taking the exam." Lisa didn't bother to lower her voice when she added, "Those morons can barely spell. You've seen their reports. A fifth-grader could do better."

"Lisa." Annie glanced around, hoping no one overheard, although everyone in the precinct pretty much felt the same way about the pair. "Look, you like being a beat cop, so why can't you understand that I like being a beat cop, too?"

"Because I know you better than that."

Annie made a point of checking her watch. "Your shift started three minutes ago."

Lisa gathered her dark blond hair back into a ponytail and secured it while getting to her feet. "Who's supposed to make dinner?"

"Why do you always ask that when it's your turn?"

Lisa grinned. "Just in case you forgot."

"O'Brien. This isn't a day at the spa." Rick Thomas, Lisa's partner, motioned impatiently.

Lisa motioned back. It wasn't nice. Then she turned once more to Annie. "I'll probably bring home takeout tonight."

"Not cheeseburgers again, please."

"Fine."

Annie watched Lisa go, looking trim and sharp in her crisp blue uniform. Lisa was one of those disgusting women who ate anything yet never gained an ounce. And it was tough being her roommate because she tended to bring home junk food that was hard to resist.

Annie got up for more coffee, weaving between the desks that crowded the room, and trying not to yawn as she passed Captain Hansen's office. After working nights for almost five years, it was hard to get used to the day shift. But she needed the switch in order to take a couple of night classes she'd been lusting after. Sadly, continuing education was the highlight of her social life.

Annie cursed under her breath when she saw that someone had drained the coffee but hadn't started another pot. She measured out the grounds and filled the carafe with water. While she waited for the coffee to brew, she stared at the calendar that hung nearby on the wall.

Monday's date was circled, marking the deadline for the detectives exam. As if she needed the reminder. Besides Lisa jumping down her throat, Mr. O'Brien had mentioned it, and her own captain had pointed out that she'd be foolish to pass up any more career opportunities.

So she'd missed the first sergeant's exam. Not on purpose. She'd been finishing her master's degree and had to study for a final. And why was everyone so worried about her career anyway? It was none of their business. If she wanted to stay where she was, that was her decision.

"Corrigan!"

She stuck her head out of the coffee room and saw Lieutenant Potter standing at her desk, Annie's phone in his hand.

"Call for you," he said, and set the receiver down on her desk.

Annoyed, she grabbed her empty mug and headed for the phone. She hoped it wasn't another personal call, particularly from her father, even though everyone in the precinct already knew about her deadbeat dad. They knew about Steve Witherspoon, too, about how the scumbag attorney had used her. That stung more than anything else.

Hell, her colleagues seemed to know everything about everybody. The precinct was like a soap opera. That's why she mostly kept to herself or hung out with Lisa.

She picked up the receiver and barked her last name.

"Annie?" The voice was shaky, but unmistakable.

"Aunt Marjorie?"

"Good heavens, girl. I hope you don't always answer the phone that way."

Annie sank into her chair, dread clawing at her chest as she glanced at the clock. Six-ten in the morning, Texas time. "Is everything okay?"

"Right as rain." Her aunt hesitated. "Except for one small thing… Honey, you got any vacation time saved up?"

"What is it, Aunt Marjorie?"

"You know I wouldn't ask you unless it was important."

"Please tell me."

Aunt Marjorie paused, her faint breath as weak as a fall leaf. "My doctor insists on me having some silly tests. Can't be done locally, of course, so I gotta go all the way to Houston."

Annie immediately picked up a pen and turned over a piece of used paper. "What kind of tests?"

"For my heart and lungs. Which are both obviously working fine or else I wouldn't be here talking to you, would I?"

Annie smiled. Aunt Marjorie had always been feisty. She was close to eighty-five, a widow for fifty-one years and as stubborn as a woman who'd lived alone so long could be. Annie adored her. "The doctor had to have a reason, Aunt Marjorie. Would you mind if I spoke to him?"

"The thing is, honey, what I really need is for you to watch my ranch. Only for a week or so, until I get out of this place. I'm worried about the chickens mostly."

"The hospital? You're there? Now?"

"Just got here," Aunt Marjorie said sheepishly. "But don't go jumping to any conclusions—you get your exercise some other way, young lady. I'm fine. It's the ranch I'm worried about. I don't want the animals starving."

"You don't have that many left, do you?"

"A few milk cows. About two dozen hens that are still laying."

"What about Chester?" Annie asked, who was already planning to go straight to the hospital and not the ranch. Chester had been an extra pair of hands and a good friend to Marjorie as far back as Annie could remember. He could take care of the few animals that remained.

"Honey, his arthritis is bad and he's no spring chicken anymore."

Annie sighed. From what she could recall, the man was at least a good eight to ten years younger than Aunt Marjorie. "Look, I'm coming to the hospital and then I'll—"

"Annie, listen. I need you at the ranch. Not here. Dang it." The beeping of medical machinery in the background made Annie's heart race. "I have to go now."

"No, wait. What hospital are you—"

She heard a click and then a dial tone. Cursing under her breath, she reached for a phone book. First, she'd book a flight, then tell the captain she needed time off. Chester would know what hospital Aunt

Marjorie was in. If not, she could ask Lisa to find out, even if she had to use official channels.

Annie's gaze caught on the piece of paper she held. An application for the detectives exam. Potter had apparently brought it over when he answered her phone. She exhaled slowly as she crumpled it in her fist and tossed it in the wastebasket. Aunt Marjorie was far more important.

LUKE MCCALL HAD had a lot of practice sneaking in and out of places and he was damn good at it. He coasted his pickup into the empty parking lot to a space right in front of the Quick Trip, turned off the engine and glanced around as he flexed his stiff shoulder. Frowning at the pain, he slowly climbed out of the truck.

At eleven o'clock, the convenience store was dead, just as he'd hoped. Instead of going straight to Hasting's Corner, he was here for supplies forty miles outside of town. Once he got to his granddad's ranch, he'd be able to hole up for a while without anyone knowing he was back. Not that anyone cared about him, except out of pure nosiness—aside from Sally Jo, who'd bring over her chicken and dumplings and an open invitation to wash more than his jeans.

And if Barb's husband was away on roundup, she'd probably show up, too. Not that Luke would ever drop his bucket in another guy's well. Even a no-account like him had some principles.

He snorted at the irony of his predicament. He

wouldn't have so much as sniffed around Joanne if he'd known she was Old Man Seabrook's wife. Hell, she was young enough to be his daughter. Easy mistake. Turned out to be a big one, though. Because now Luke had the law crawling up his ass. The kind of money Seabrook had could buy a whole lot of trouble for Luke.

He pushed open the door, setting off the overhead bell and, without looking up from the paper she was scribbling on, the woman behind the counter said, "We just closed."

Luke removed his Stetson, and swept back his hair, just as the woman looked up. "Sorry, ma'am. I must've missed the sign."

She blinked, then shoved a pencil behind her ear and gave him a quick once-over. A slow smile lifted her ruby-red lips. "Well, cowboy, you go ahead and lock that door behind you and I'll give you time to get what you come for."

Luke tipped his hat to her before resetting it on his head. "Thank you, ma'am." His smile vanished as soon as he turned away to lock the door. Must be getting old. He used to like being gawked at as if he were a piece of juicy chicken-fried steak.

"Won't be but a minute," he said and strolled down the aisle toward the refrigerated section, feeling the weight of her stare at his back.

"Take your time," she called after him. "I'm just wrapping up my paperwork, and it'll be nice to have a big strong man walk me out to my car for a change."

Luke blew out a puff of air. Walking out with her was all he was doing. He grabbed a six-pack of beer from the refrigerator, reconsidered, and exchanged it for a twelve-pack. If he was lucky, maybe he could hide out at the deserted old ranch for a week before the sheriff found out that he had inherited the place six months ago. Careful of his injured shoulder, he carried the beer, three packages of cold cuts and two loaves of bread to the register.

"You going to a party?" the woman asked, eyeing his haul.

"No, ma'am." He withdrew his wallet and waited for her to ring up his purchases.

"You call me ma'am one more time, cowboy, and I'll have to spank you." Her teasing grin made one side of his mouth hike up. "I'm not that much older than you." She dropped his lunchmeat and bread into a bag. "But don't you worry. I got a husband and two nearly grown boys of my own, but I can still look."

"You best be careful, ma—, uh, darlin'," he said. "It's late, the place is deserted. You shouldn't be talking to a strange man like that."

She took the money he handed her. "Thought you might be from around here, but I guess not. This is East Texas, sugar. Anyway, I ain't got nothing to worry about with you." She winked as she handed him his change. "It's all in your eyes. Decent men have that certain look."

Luke snorted. Boy, she had no idea how wrong she was. All she had to do was ask anyone in Hasting's

Corner. Luke's own grandfather could have set her straight if the ornery old buzzard hadn't keeled over last year while trying to shoe a stubborn mule. "You ready for that escort outside?" he asked, gathering up his groceries.

She smiled. "You go on ahead, handsome. I still have another ten minutes of trying to make some sense out of these here numbers."

Luke hesitated, but she came around the counter to shoo him out, getting to the door before him to unlock it.

Her gaze caught on his belt buckle, the one he'd won three years ago. "Hey, you on the circuit?"

He nodded, anxious to leave before she asked any more questions. Too late, he realized. He should have just lied and said it belonged to his brother.

"You somebody I would know?"

"Nah."

"Well, you won that buckle. That's no small thing. What's your name?"

"Tom Black."

"Hmm, we're big rodeo fans. But I can't say I recall your name. Sorry."

"No problem. I'm new to the circuit."

Her disbelieving frown was like a bucket of cold water thrown in his face. Hell, he already knew he was getting too old to still be riding, much less be new to the game.

"Well, you drive careful, you hear?" she said, then opened the door and locked it behind him. His arms full, he nudged his chin in farewell when she waved, then deposited his groceries and himself into the battered white pickup.

Slouching down in the seat, he adjusted his hat and was surprised by a fleeting image of his grandfather. Luke missed him sometimes. The guy could be as stern and dour as a lemon-sucking preacher, but he was still the only father Luke had ever known. His own daddy had skipped town before Luke had taken his first step. Didn't want no kids, no responsibility, he'd told everyone, then just up and left.

Now that he was older, Luke understood. He didn't like being tied down, either, but he sure as hell wouldn't leave a wife and baby behind to starve. Nope. The rodeo was his life and he made no apologies. And he sure as hell didn't scatter regrets.

One by one the lights went out in the store and then the door opened and Luke straightened. He watched the clerk hurry toward a blue compact car and open the door, before he started his truck.

Once she was safely inside and had turned on her headlights, he put the truck in gear. She honked and waved as she reversed out of the stall. He pulled out onto the highway and headed toward Hasting's Corner, not sure what he was going to do once he got there, besides sleep. He needed a solid twenty-four hours' worth. Then, maybe he could come up with a plan to get to Joanne.

Then, too, if he laid low long enough, maybe Seabrook would cool off and admit that Luke hadn't stolen the million bucks in prize money. He flexed his aching shoulder, wincing with the pain that shot to his neck. Hell, even if it took a month to straighten out this mess, it wasn't as if he'd be getting on another bull soon. Not till Houston, anyway. For the money. Even if it ended up being the last time. The hell with what the doctors said.

He got to the familiar fork in the road and veered right toward Hasting's Corner. The road, narrow and full of potholes, divided the flat idle land for endless miles. Without streetlights and with no moon it was too dark to see anything, but he remembered the road well, even though he'd only been back twice since he'd left home at sixteen.

The farther it went the land got hilly and more interesting. That's where that bastard Seabrook lived. In a big white show-house on the side of a hill, facing a lake. The self-proclaimed king of the rodeo, big and mean as a Brahma bull, Seabrook ruled the county. And wasn't it just Luke's rotten luck that of all the counties this side of Texas, the bastard had to live here?

Something flashed up ahead. Luke caught it right before he rounded the bend. It was a car, still distant, but no mistaking the warning lights.

"Damn!"

He slowed down, trying to decide if he should stop. Ten miles out of town like this, it could be someone he knew.

"Damn!"

Whoever it was had to have a cell phone. Everyone did these days and, if not, ten miles wasn't that far to walk. He got close enough to see that it was a small red Ford, its right rear tire stuck in a ditch. But no sign of a person. Good. Problem solved.

Just as he passed the car he saw her—a woman, slim, with long, dark, wavy hair. Standing in the beam of the headlights.

"Damn." He couldn't leave her out here.

But then again…

He turned the truck around.

2

"DAMN IT!"

Annie slapped at the fourth mosquito that had assailed her in the past two minutes, and watched the truck speed by. Too bad she didn't have her gun. She'd shoot the dumb tires. Before she could get her purse and start hoofing it toward town, she saw the truck turn around.

She sighed with relief. Although the driver could be an axe murderer. Terrific thought. Nah, this was Texas hill country, not Brooklyn. Not that she was foolish enough not to worry some. But walking for ten miles in the dark didn't seem smart, either.

The white pickup coasted to a stop beside her. She couldn't see the driver until he reached over and opened the passenger door. The interior light was dim, but not enough to shadow his vivid blue eyes.

"Seems you have a problem, darlin'," he said in a slow easy drawl. His sexy smile gave her a shiver where it had no business.

"I don't suppose you'd be able to give me a tow out of that ditch."

"Nope. Too dark. And I don't have any rope. But I can give you a ride to town. Got two gas stations there."

"Open at this time of night?"

"Nope. Hop in."

"Give me a minute to get my bag." By the time she opened the car door, he'd gotten out of his truck and met her there. His right shoulder brushed across her breasts as he beat her to the bag sitting on the back seat.

"You travel mighty light for a woman," he said as he hauled out the black nylon overnighter. "That's refreshing."

"That's sexist."

"Just speaking from experience." He gave her one of those sexy smiles again.

Her left calf tickled as if something had crawled up under her jeans. Probably nothing, but she leaned down and rubbed through the denim anyway. "I'm Annie Corrigan, by the way."

He hesitated. "Luke. Where you headed?"

"Hasting's Corner. Well, actually to my aunt's ranch on the other side of town."

"What's her name?"

"Marjorie Wilson."

"Oh, yeah, the widow woman."

"You know her?"

Either he hadn't heard her or he chose to ignore the question. He opened the truck's passenger door and waited until she climbed in, then closed it before stowing her bag in the back and getting behind the wheel.

"She's in the hospital," Annie said. "Having some tests done."

"Sorry to hear that."

"So you live around here?"

"Used to." That's all he said.

Fine with Annie. She didn't feel like talking, either. She was tired, sticky hot from the humidity, and a little worried about what she'd find when she got to the ranch. She knew it wasn't a big production. From what she remembered, besides the cows and chickens and a few stray dogs, Aunt Marjorie sometimes used to board horses. Hopefully, Chester had everything under control. It wasn't as if Annie could do much, unless given direction.

God, she should've ignored Aunt Marjorie and headed straight for Houston. She should've called Chester from there, made sure everything was all right and then gone to be with her aunt. Generally, she was more rational than this acting first and thinking later business. Of course, it wouldn't be too late to go to Houston in the morning. Provided she got the dumb rental car out of the ditch.

She glanced over at Luke. He kept his gaze on the road, his brows slightly puckered. His mind was definitely somewhere else. Maybe she'd made him late for something. Probably a hook up; he was a real hottie. Perfect eyes, perfect lips, the lower one fuller than the top one, just the way she liked them.

And, oh, mama, she'd seen the way he filled out those faded jeans. With his hat and cowboy boots, he definitely had the whole thing going on. Lisa would have been all over him by now.

"I really appreciate you stopping," she said, after staring at him for too long. "I'd been standing there a while."

He looked over at her, almost as if he'd forgotten that she was sitting there. How flattering. Then he gave her a lazy, sexy smile and all was forgotten. "No problem, darlin'. Happy to help a pretty lady in distress."

"Oh, brother."

He cocked a brow at her.

She coyly put a hand to her mouth. "Oops. Did I say that out loud?"

His lips curved and then he laughed, a full rich sound that resonated in the cab of the truck and warmed her in uncomfortably intimate places.

She turned back to the road and gripped the dashboard. "Look out!"

Caught by the headlights, a deer stood frozen in the middle of the road. Luke swerved, but clipped the animal on the hind end. It started to dart but fell to the pavement.

"Shit!" He stopped the truck, threw it into Park and got out.

The doe got to her feet and then dropped her hind end again.

Annie climbed out behind Luke who'd already knelt beside the animal.

"Steady, girl," he whispered. "Let's take a look here."

The deer jerked, and tried again to get up.

"What can I do?" Annie asked.

He ignored her, his attention solely on the doe. He gently touched the animal's flank and whispered something Annie couldn't hear. The doe seemed to calm down enough for him to probe her leg, his large tanned hand stroking the area, prompting a surprisingly lusty reaction from Annie.

His fingers were long and lean, his nails clean and nicely squared off. Easy to imagine them roaming over a woman's body. Her body. She cleared her throat.

At the sound, the doe started. Then she leaped to her feet and darted into the trees.

Luke got up just as suddenly, and Annie didn't have time to step out of his way. To keep them from colliding, she put a hand on his shoulder. As he straightened, her palm slid down his forearm. Firm rounded muscles lay beneath the blue Western-cut shirt. The man was definitely athletic. She let go, hoping her reluctance didn't show too much.

He dusted his jeans and stared after the deer even though she'd disappeared. "She's bruised a little, but stunned more than anything else. She'll be okay." He lifted his hat and swept a hand through his longish sun-streaked hair before setting the hat back on his head. "If she stays off the road, that is."

Annie followed him back to the truck. "That was amazing how she calmed down for you."

"She knew I was no threat."

"How?"

He put the truck back in drive. "Around these parts, I'm known as the deer whisperer."

"Really?"

After a brief silence, he burst out laughing. "Where are you from?"

Heat rushed to her cheeks. Damn it. She was a good cop because of her good instincts. No one would ever dare consider her gullible. "And here I was just starting to think you were a nice guy."

"Don't make that mistake." He stretched his neck from side to side, grimacing with the effort, and then tipped his hat back slightly. "We'll be hitting town in a couple of minutes. Guess you want to go straight to your aunt's place."

"If you don't mind."

"Nope. You got any folks there that can give you a ride in to town tomorrow?"

Annie rested her aching head back against the seat. Today had been only her third time on a plane. She hated it. Way too stressful. After today, if she never left New York again that would be fine with her. "I don't think so. Maybe Chester."

Luke let out a laugh. "That old buzzard's still kicking, huh?"

Annie snorted. "What a nice way to put it."

He shrugged his good shoulder. "I've known the old guy since I was knee high to a mule. He and my granddad used to play cards every Saturday night. Made me fetch their beer and chewing tobacco when they ran out."

"Is that where you're going? To visit your grandfather?"

His mouth tightened. "He passed almost a year ago."

"I'm sorry."

Luke gave an abrupt nod, then made it clear he didn't want to talk anymore by rolling down his window and staring hard off into the darkness. "I'm gonna make a quick detour. Won't take but a minute."

She should have been scared, or at least concerned. She didn't know this man. But her gut told her it was okay and she always trusted her gut. Except when it came to men and it was personal—then her instincts sucked. The fiasco with Steve Witherspoon was proof enough.

They turned down a dark side road, mostly gravel judging by the crunching of the tires. But they'd only driven a few feet when Luke stopped the truck and muttered a soft curse.

"What's wrong?"

Shaking his head, he squinted hard toward the glow of a faint light filtering through the trees. Without a word, he threw the truck into Reverse and sped backward all the way to the main road.

She clutched the armrest and held her breath. It was so dark. Only a sliver of moon was visible. He couldn't possibly see where he was going. He swung backward onto the highway and her stomach lurched. And tourists complained about New York cabbies.

"What is going on?"

"Nothing."

"Yeah, I could tell." After nearly sliding off the seat, she straightened. He ignored her, keeping his eyes steady on the road, his mind obviously preoccupied.

She respected his apparent need for silence, but another careless move like that and she'd get out and walk. And then he could have all the silence he wanted.

As soon as her heart-rate returned to normal, she focused on the task ahead of her. Halfway through the small town she realized where they were. It was easy to miss without any lights on. In fact, there wasn't even a single streetlight.

"Man, the place hasn't changed a bit," Luke murmured with a hint of disdain.

"How long has it been since you've been back?"

"A while."

Annie didn't push. God knew she understood if he didn't want to talk about his family. Now that she was older, it didn't smart as much but, as a child, when the subject of parents came up, all she wanted to do was crawl into a dark corner and hide. How did you tell other kids or their parents that your dad was a drunk and spent more time in jail than out? Or have to confess that your mother hadn't wanted to be a mother after all, and had run off to Hollywood to seek the fame that she never found?

"You're quiet," Luke said finally.

"I didn't think you wanted to talk."

"Doesn't matter. We're here."

She sat up straighter and peered into the darkness. A red reflector on the mailbox pole caught her eye. Other than that, there was no indication this was her aunt's place, or that any house existed nearby. But catching sight of a funny shaped tree that was briefly illuminated by the headlights helped her recognize the place.

The first summer she'd visited the ranch she'd gotten in trouble for swinging on its lower branches. She'd fallen and sprained her right ankle, and scared Aunt Marjorie senseless.

The truck hit a pothole and Annie's teeth came down hard on her lower lip. She bit back an oath and then kept her teeth clamped shut. In less than a minute they got to the gate, which seemed pointless since the fencing had come down in at least three places, but that's all Annie could see.

A floodlight coming from the eaves of the barn cast a dim light on the gravel road that led to the house. Everything looked horribly dingy, and Annie prayed it was because of the poor lighting. It had to be. Aunt Marjorie had money. She'd paid for Annie's college tuition. Her books. The dorm. She'd paid for everything.

The closer they got to the house, the deeper Annie's heart sank. The place was a mess. Lighting had nothing to do with the sagging front porch or the chipped white paint that had once made the railings and picket fence seem like part of a fairy tale to Annie's bruised young heart.

"How long has she been in the hospital?" Luke

asked as he stopped the truck in front of the cracked walk.

Annie sighed. "I had no idea that— Oh!" But she would have, if she hadn't been so self-absorbed. Aunt Marjorie was almost eighty-five. She couldn't take care of the place, not with only Chester's help. But why hadn't she hired more hands? Had she blown all her savings on Annie? The thought made Annie sick. Bile rose in her throat.

"You okay?"

She turned to find him watching her. Unfortunately, what little light there was shone on their faces. "Thanks for the ride. I really appreciate this," she said, reaching for the door handle.

He peered closer, frowning, and then touched the side of her jaw, forcing her to turn her chin toward him. "What happened here?"

Reflexively, she jerked away from his touch and felt her chin. "What?"

"Here." He touched the corner of her mouth and his finger came away with a blood smear.

"Oh, the pothole. I bit my lip."

He grimaced. "Sorry, darlin'. I was trying to take it easy."

"It's nothing." Hell, she'd even been shot once. The bullet had only grazed her, but she still had a small scar on her thigh.

"You just wait now." He drew his finger across her lip. "I don't want Chester coming at me with a shotgun."

Her gaze was drawn to the curve of his mouth, the

way his shadowed chin dimpled ever so slightly. His voice was so low and intimate that she had to swallow before speaking.

"Aunt Marjorie said he still sleeps in the bunkhouse." Her voice came out a whisper, the innocent words sounding, even to her, like an invitation. But once they were uttered, she held her breath waiting for his response.

"Well, then how are you gonna get in the house short of waking him up?" He'd moved his hand away from her mouth but kept his arm resting along the back of the seat.

"I know where the key's hidden."

"Ah, the hidden key." He grinned, his teeth gleaming, his hat hiding his eyes. His beard-rough skin almost disguised the scar that curved up the side of his jaw.

"Well, thanks again for the lift." She pulled the door handle but it wouldn't move.

He leaned across her with his left arm, his chest brushing her breasts, his rough chin grazing her skin, and he jerked the handle. "Gets stuck sometimes," he said, his mouth close enough to hers that, if she moved a fraction of an inch, they'd touch. Then he pushed the door open, his arms practically encircling her. "There you go."

"Thanks," she murmured, and held still as he unhurriedly drew back, the warmth of his breath lingering seductively on her cheek. When she could finally breathe, she slid out of the truck.

Luke got out, too, and grabbed her bag.

"You don't have to—"

"I'm not letting you walk into a dark house unescorted. Now, you go on and find that key. I'll turn my back if you want."

She snorted, tempted to tell him she was a Brooklyn cop and could take care of herself. But part of her didn't want him to leave, or want to find out that he was one of those guys who ran from the uniform. Not that it mattered. He'd be gone in a matter of minutes. So, what would it hurt if she let him walk her inside? Let him think she was scared. So what?

Luke kept the truck's headlights on while she climbed the rickety front steps, carefully sidestepping a rotting board. She found the key taped under a carved wooden blue jay perched on top of a homemade bird feeder, just where Aunt Marjorie said it would be. The lock stuck at first but, after jiggling it, the door opened, and she found the porch light switch.

As bad as the place initially looked, under the light the appalling amount of disrepair sickened Annie. Not just cosmetic stuff, either. The porch was actually sagging in the middle, frighteningly near where Aunt Marjorie kept her scarred oak rocking chair.

"Looks like Mrs. Walker's been sick for a while." Luke had come up behind her.

Embarrassed to admit she didn't know, Annie reached for her bag. "Really, I can take it from here. I don't want to inconvenience you any more than I already have."

He held the bag out of her reach and gave her a crooked smile. "You wouldn't be trying to get rid of me now, would you?"

"Yes."

Surprise lifted his brows and he laughed. "That's just too bad," he said then carried the bag into the house.

It took Annie a moment to follow. His reaction surprised her, and she wasn't sure how to take his persistence. But her eyes helplessly kept pace with him. He was one fine looking man.

She pulled herself together and caught up with him in the living room. The sight of the worn blue carpet and faded upholstered furniture brought her back to reality. She swallowed hard. Only two years ago, Aunt Marjorie had sent her a check toward graduate school tuition. Annie had refused at first but her aunt had insisted, claiming that she had nothing else to spend her money on.

Annie muttered a curse under her breath. How could she have been so selfish? If she'd only taken the time to visit in the past five years….

"Hey."

She looked at Luke. "What?"

"You okay?"

"Fine."

"Right." He looked around, then held up the bag. "Where do you want me to put this?"

"Anywhere." She shook her head. "I'll take it." The place was worn but couldn't be neater. The least she could do was to keep it that way.

He let go of the bag but she didn't like the way he studied her, as if trying to figure out what was going on inside her head. "I sure could use something cold to drink," he said before she could figuratively show him the door.

"I'm not sure what's available—"

"Water would be fine."

She could hardly refuse. She set the bag on the brown corduroy recliner and started to go right, and then realized the kitchen was the other way. He followed, not bothering to hide his interest in the place, checking out the chipped windowsills and cracked kitchen linoleum.

Silly for her to take it personally, but she did. By the time she got to the refrigerator, her annoyance had escalated. She owed him something to drink at the very least. Maybe she should even offer him some money for his time, and then she'd politely explain that she was exhausted. Anybody would get the hint and leave.

She found some orange juice and a jug of iced tea, and then she got out a tray of ice. It took a couple of tries before she found the cupboard that held glasses, a collection of mismatched tumblers and a set of tall pastel plastic ones. She heard a funny click and turned around.

Luke stood there with the blade of his army knife extended toward her.

3

ANNIE'S GAZE FIXED on the knife. "What are you doing?"

Too late, Luke realized how it must look. He picked up the kitchen chair and turned it upside down. "This thing is a little shaky. Figure it needed some tightening."

"Oh." She blinked, then looked at him with relief in her eyes. "Thanks."

"Happy to help." This setup was perfect. Luke smiled at Annie. She was cute in an earthy sort of way. With her long untamed brown hair and wide hazel eyes with barely any makeup, she reminded him of a girl he'd hung out with in high school, in fact the only dark-haired girl he'd ever dated. And that had been only the once. After going to a movie, and then making out under the bleachers at the football stadium, they'd ended up being more like buddies. Until he'd skipped town.

He finished the task of tightening two of the legs, his mind racing. Obviously he couldn't go back to his granddad's ranch. Seabrook's hired guns shouldn't have figured it out and found the place so quickly. Luke had underestimated them. But staying in a motel around these parts was out of the question. He might as well take out an ad in the local paper telling them where he was. Yet he needed to stay close, to find a way to get to Joanne.

Annie Corrigan didn't know it yet, but she was the answer to his problem. He set the chair to rights and smiled at her. "Have a seat, darlin'."

Frowning slightly, she set a glass of what looked like apple juice on the table, or maybe it was Scotch. Either one was all right with him. "You go ahead," she said.

"Anything wrong?" He removed his hat and set it on the table as he slid onto the chair.

"What? Oh, no, I was just—it's nothing."

He nodded, picked up the glass, smelled the apple juice and sipped its icy sweetness. He'd have much preferred scotch or better yet, beer, but for now, he needed to keep a wholesome impression. "You know if Chester's still driving?"

"Not a clue." She poured herself a glass, and he helped himself to a good look at the generous curve of her backside.

He looked up as soon as she turned around. "To-morrow morning, I'll get that car of yours out of the ditch."

She looked torn. "I don't want to inconvenience you any more than—"

"You can cook me breakfast. How's that?"

She sighed, briefly closing her eyes and rubbing

her right temple. "Then you'll have to take me to the store to get groceries, and I'll owe you again."

Like hell, he'd go into town. He smiled. "Cheer up."

"Right." Her gaze went from the cracked linoleum floor to the yellow refrigerator that had to be over fifteen years old. "Have you taken a good look at this place?"

"Not your responsibility, is it?"

"Uh, yeah, it is, sort of," she said, abruptly looking away. "It's complicated."

"So you're gonna be fixing it up?"

She turned back to him, her lips parting, but nothing came out. Her shoulders sagged, and finally she said, "Yes."

"Then you're in luck. Just so happens I'm between jobs. For room and board, I'm all yours."

"Really?"

"Do with me as you please, ma'am."

Her lips twitched. "That's quite an offer."

Luke smiled. "You don't know the half of it."

She breathed in, her breasts expanding beneath her thin white cotton shirt. "Are you sure about this? It seems like the place needs an awful lot of work."

"I can't promise to get it all done, but I'll do what I can in the next ten days."

"Fair enough. But I insist on paying you something, as well."

"No need. A roof over my head and grub in my belly is plenty."

She frowned suddenly. "Wait a minute. You have a place near here."

"Yeah, well, the thing is…" He cleared his throat. He knew the question was bound to come up, but he didn't have an easy answer without sounding like a whipped dog. "I haven't been back for a while, and the place is a mess."

"Wouldn't it make more sense to concentrate on getting *your* place in shape?"

He scrubbed at his face. How many questions was this woman gonna ask?

"Not that I wouldn't appreciate the help…" Curiosity brought out the golden flecks in her eyes.

"Look, when I say I haven't been back in a while, I'm talking a long time," he muttered and saw that her interest hadn't died any. "It's complicated," he said, echoing her earlier words.

She sat there quietly for a moment, her thoughts clearly somewhere else, and then said, "Got it." She stuck out her hand. "You have a deal."

He stared at her hand for a moment. It wasn't that he didn't understand the gesture, but damn, he didn't know any women who shook hands. They hugged, they kissed, some of them even pinched his ass, but they didn't shake hands. Not that this was a bad thing. Just different.

"Um, something wrong?"

"Nope." He slid his palm against her warm soft flesh. "Deal."

"Good."

Neither of them moved for several moments. She withdrew her hand first, took a quick sip of the juice she'd poured for herself and then got up.

He leaned back in the chair and watched her. Staying here with her wouldn't be a hardship. No, sir. She was on the thin side, with small breasts, but that nice round backside more than made up for anything lacking up front. Not that he was an ass man. He just liked women, period. Always found something nice about each and every one of them. Got him in trouble enough times, that was for sure.

She turned suddenly, but he didn't think she'd caught him checking her out. He hadn't been that obvious. She opened the refrigerator again and then one of the cupboards. "You must be hungry," she said, and went to another cupboard that was almost as bare as the first. "Let's see. Canned peaches, more canned peaches and…" She got up on tiptoes to see what was on the back of the second shelf, and then sighed. "I hope you like canned peaches."

Luke smiled. "I stopped at a store on the way over and bought some stuff for sandwiches. They're in the cooler in the back of my truck." He got to his feet. "I'll go get it."

"Go ahead and take it to the bunkhouse with you."

"The bunkhouse?"

"Yeah."

"Darlin', I'm not sleeping in the bunkhouse. I'm sleeping here with you."

"With me?" Her eyebrows arched in amusement. "You think so?"

He tried not to smile. He didn't mean it like it sounded. He just wanted to stay in the house. "I'm cheap labor. Don't I deserve a nice soft bed?"

She leaned a hip against the counter and folded her arms across her chest. "I'm sure Chester can accommodate you."

"Come on now, darlin'."

Her expression tightened. "Don't take this wrong, okay, but I—"

"I know what you're gonna say, and I don't blame you for mistrusting me. A girl can't be too careful and all that, but if I'd wanted to—"

"I'm not worried that you're going to attack me," Annie said, cutting him off. "I simply don't like you calling me darlin'."

"Why?"

She looked at him as if he'd crawled out from under a rock. "It's demeaning."

He thought for a moment. Hell, nowadays you couldn't call them *ma'am* or *darlin'* without getting your head bitten off. "Well, I figured I knew what that word meant, but now I'm not so sure. Just trying to be friendly is all." He gave her his winning smile, she only rolled her eyes. "Maybe you should *be* more worried about letting a strange man into the house alone with you."

She laughed. "Trust me. I can take care of myself," she said, watching him closely. Too closely for his liking. "I'm a cop. A New York police officer. Brooklyn to be exact."

That took the wind out of him. "A cop?"

She nodded.

"A cop," he repeated, mostly to himself, hoping this was a really bad joke.

"Yep. Sergeant Annie Corrigan."

Damn.

"YOU FIND THAT no-good son of a bitch yet?"

Sheriff Jethro Wilcox held the cell phone away from his ear. Ernest Seabrook was loud enough when he wasn't pissed off and, for the past two days, the man had been madder than a rutting buck without a doe.

"Not yet, Mr. Seabrook, but I figure he'll show up at his granddaddy's old ranch soon enough."

"Soon enough?" Seabrook hollered. "Soon enough? Yesterday couldn't have been goddamn soon enough. You understanding me, Jethro?"

"Yes, sir." No use pointing out that was merely a figure of speech. The old man was as hardheaded as he was obnoxious, but he paid mighty well and it wouldn't serve any purpose to piss him off further.

"You get me my million bucks, you hear? And you bring me that son of a bitch."

No kidding. Why else would he be sitting out here by the McCall ranch, sweating like a pig in the heat and humidity near a mosquito-infested pond? "Yes, sir." One of the critters buzzed near his ear. He swatted, missed and cursed.

"What did you say to me, boy?" Seabrook's voice came out in an angry wheeze and then he started coughing. More than likely caused by the stinky cigars he was always smoking.

Wilcox smiled. "Nothing, Mr. Seabrook. Just getting eaten alive by these friggin' mosquitoes."

"Well, the sooner you find Luke McCall, the sooner you can go home." Seabrook severed the connection.

Wilcox flipped his cell closed and slipped it into the breast pocket of his uniform shirt. He could go home any time he damn well pleased. Technically he didn't work for Seabrook, but he'd gotten himself knee-deep in debt to the bastard, which, around these parts, pretty much meant Seabrook owned his ass.

What he couldn't figure out was why Joanne stayed with that nasty piece of lard. Yeah, he had money, but she was a mighty fine looking woman and half his age. She could find another sugar daddy over in Dallas. A woman like that would be taken care of for a long time if she was so inclined.

Another mosquito buzzed close to his ear. He swatted at it, slapping the back of his sunburned neck too hard. "Son of a bitch." He stared through the trees toward the highway. Couldn't see a damn thing. Twenty minutes ago he'd seen headlights, but it must have been a wrong turn. Besides, the lights were high and wide like a truck's, not like McCall's flashy red Corvette.

Jethro stretched out his legs and slid lower in the seat so that the back of his head hit the headrest. If McCall didn't show up tonight or early tomorrow morning, Jethro's guess was that the guy had hopped a plane in Dallas. If Jethro had stolen a million dollars, that's what he would've done. Get the hell out of Dodge, pronto. The only reason he was sitting in this crummy place at all was on account of Seabrook's stubborn belief that McCall wouldn't leave the state. Or the county, for that matter.

The whole thing just didn't add up. Seabrook was president of the stockmen's association that put up rodeo prize money. Luke McCall was one of the top bull riders in the country. Over his career, he'd earned over a million dollars and, as long in the tooth as that ole boy was getting, he was still riding. More than likely he would've taken a nice chunk of that prize money at next month's rodeo. So why steal the mil? And what had he been doing at Seabrook's ranch anyway?

There was no love lost between those two. Not since the Fourth of July two years ago, when Seabrook spooked Luke's horse real bad right before the rodeo started. Some folks thought the old man had done it on purpose. If Luke had hurt himself he wouldn't have ridden that big mean Samson. Staying on that Brahma bull for a record time ended up winning Luke a fifty-thousand-dollar purse.

Still, that missing money didn't mean anything to Seabrook. Only a portion of it was his contribution to the stockmen's association and it wasn't out of the goodness of their hearts they put up the prize money. It was all promotion. They got back large returns that made blowhards like Seabrook millionaires.

Maybe Luke grabbed the cash to get even with Seabrook. Although that didn't seem like McCall's style. Or maybe he just wanted to make Seabrook sweat for a while. The old man was obviously embarrassed. That's why he wanted the whole mess kept under wraps.

Jethro adjusted his hat to partially cover his eyes but still allow him to see if any headlights appeared. Seabrook had offered to square his debt if he brought Luke back and, no matter what their beef, that's exactly what Jethro aimed to do.

WELL, HE DIDN'T RUN, but he sure looked as if he wanted to. Annie poured herself a second glass of juice. Her mouth had gotten so dry it felt as if her tongue had swollen. "You want another one?"

Luke shook his head. "If you don't mind, I think I'll go get a beer out of my cooler."

"Knock yourself out." She'd bet next month's rent that he'd get in his truck and she'd never see him again. The horrified look on his face when she told him she was a cop took first place as far as reactions went.

"Want one?"

"Sure." She waited until he got to the back door and said, "You forgot your hat."

He turned and stared at it for a moment, and then his eyes met hers and his mouth curved up on one side. "I didn't forget it."

She watched him leave, and then she moved to the window to watch him walk to his truck. Yeah, he made a great picture with his long legs and snug-fitting jeans. Broad shoulders, for which she was a hopeless sucker, that tapered to a narrow waist made him look like he should be in a commercial.

She was equally interested in the way he walked. His long leisurely strides told her more about the man than he had himself. It was her job to study people, to understand the small quirks or habits that gave them away. So far, Luke had shown her two things: confidence and compassion, an interesting combination in a male ego. Healthy certainly, but really surprising at his age and the way he looked.

He had to be in his early thirties, and had to receive oodles of female attention. Probably got by on charm more than anything else. He certainly wasn't lacking in that department. Even though Annie hated gratuitous endearments, she knew enough women who ate them up.

Tomorrow she'd have to ask Aunt Marjorie about him, or even ask Chester for that matter. She'd left the barn door wide-open already, as they'd say around here. She knew well enough she wouldn't sleep soundly with this guy in the next room. She trusted her instinct but she'd be foolish not to be a bit apprehensive.

He turned back toward the house, and she ducked away from the window, grabbed their glasses and rinsed them out. She waited until she heard him set something on the table before she turned around. He'd brought in the entire cooler, which made sense, but it was still a little weird. She'd just met him and he was practically moving in.

"I figured I ought to put this food in the refrigerator. Can't let it go bad. We might have to live on ham sandwiches for a while."

"With white bread, I bet."

"Is there any other kind?" He winked at her, and then pulled packages of cold cuts out of the cooler and deposited them into the refrigerator.

She watched him stack everything neatly on the second shelf, leaving room for the beer and a quart of milk. She thought about offering to help, but it was much more fun watching the way his shirt stretched across his back as he moved and how the soft faded denim molded his perfect ass.

His legs were long and, even without the inch heels on his cowboy boots, he was tall. Well over six feet for sure, since she was five-seven and only came up to his shoulders.

He kept out two beers. After opening them both, he handed one to her. She took it, even though she wasn't crazy about beer. Rarely did she drink alcohol, and when she did it was some sweet frothy concoction that the guys at the precinct called a girly drink.

"What's the plan for tomorrow?" Luke asked after taking a long pull.

"Get my car out."

"Right. First thing."

"Talk to Chester about repairs."

Luke pulled out a kitchen chair for her. "Don't

count on him being much help. He's always had a bum leg and, at his age—" he shook his head "—the guy shouldn't be doing too much."

"Yeah, I know." She sat down, exhaustion suddenly saturating her limbs. Not only was it late, but her body was still on East Coast time.

He took the seat across from her and leaned both elbows on the table. "He can help us figure out where the repairs are most needed and what kind of supplies are stored before we buy anything."

She'd just paid off a chunk of her credit card so she was good in that department. Of course, she had no idea how much wood and paint and fencing and those sorts of things cost. If she maxed out her credit card, she didn't care. Even that wouldn't erase the guilt she felt for accepting the tuition money.

Annie shifted positions trying to get comfortable and bumped his leg. "Sorry."

They both moved to get out of the way at the same time and bumped legs again.

Luke gave her a lopsided smile. "You keep flirting with me like this, I'll start calling you darlin' again."

"I have a gun and I know how to use it."

"Now you're getting me excited."

She laughed. "You're one sick puppy."

"I've been called worse."

"Deservedly?"

"Oh, yeah," he said matter-of-factly, and tipped the beer to his lips. Setting the bottle back on the table, he jerked and winced. His sharp intake of breath ended with a mild oath.

"What's wrong?"

He gingerly rolled his shoulder. "Got a bad bruise."

"A bruise?"

"From a fall."

She didn't say anything, just watched him probe his shoulder. A bruise wouldn't cause that much pain. Maybe he didn't want to tell her what had happened. Maybe she should start worrying.

He sighed. "You know what a rodeo is?"

"Of course."

He started to unbutton his shirt. "Let's say I met a bull more ornery than me."

Each unfastened button exposed more smooth golden brown skin. "What are you doing?"

He undid the last button and shrugged the shirt off his left shoulder. "The doc gave me some ointment that helps with the stiffness." He got a small tube out of the duffel bag beside the cooler and uncapped it. "I've dislocated it twice now and tore some ligaments last year, so now it acts up every once in a while."

"Should you have been carrying all that stuff?" she asked, nudging her chin toward the cooler, but unable to drag her gaze away from his chest.

"It didn't hurt then."

"Are you *twelve?*" Her gaze stalled on his belly where the hair arrowed downward, and then slid to the bulk behind his fly. Definitely not twelve.

Smiling, he squeezed the white goop onto his

palm. When he stretched his arm across his chest to reach the back of his shoulder, he grimaced, the pain tightening his features.

"Here." She scooped the ointment from his palm onto hers and stood behind him. After rubbing her palms together to warm them, she gently slid them across his back.

He tensed.

She withdrew.

"Don't stop."

"Tell me if I hurt you."

"I promise to cry like a baby."

She smiled and slid her palms over hard muscle and smooth skin. Wow, he was perfect. Too perfect. Her nipples tightened. She bit her lower lip, and slowly worked her fingers around his shoulder blades.

He moaned. Not like he was hurt. More like how she felt: damp between the thighs, her mouth dry as cotton. When her hands started to shake, she stepped back until he was out of reach.

Luke looked over his shoulder at her.

"Good night," she murmured, and took off down the hall.

4

LUKE WOKE UP with a hard on. Not the usual morning kind. This one was much more specific. Caused by one Annie Corrigan of the Brooklyn police department. *Sergeant* Annie Corrigan. Some luck he had.

Still, the woman was easy on the eyes and, man, those hands of hers. She might have eased the pain in his shoulder, but she'd stirred up a world of hurt in other areas. His cock twitched at the thought of her soft palms exploring his back, tracing his backbone lower than she'd needed. She had great hair, too. Long and slightly wild, its softness had brushed his bare shoulder and, for a moment, the pain was gone.

So she was a cop. She didn't have any jurisdiction or interest in what was happening way out here and, since he didn't dare go to Granddad's place, staying here was perfect. Who'd poke around way out here? From what he recalled, Marjorie Walker had been a loner since her husband passed. She didn't care for the local grapevine, so mostly stuck to herself, and Chester only went to town for supplies. Luke was pretty sure, if he asked him, the old guy wouldn't mention Luke was back.

Poor Annie had her hands full enough. She'd be too busy fixing the place up to be dawdling around town, inviting questions. Anything they needed in the way of food or paint or wood, he'd go over to Sawyer County and pick up. Some folks knew him there, but mostly on account of the rodeo.

He rolled onto his side and squinted at his watch on the antique oak nightstand that matched the narrow twin bed. It couldn't be nine already. He hadn't slept that long since his hard-drinking days. When he'd been too young and too stupid and spent too much money on flashy cars and even flashier women. Luckily, those days were gone, but so was a lot of his money. Friggin' idiot that he was.

Finally, he'd gotten his act together. He'd actually managed to save his last three winnings. And then this mess with Seabrook. Stupid bastard. Ready to ruin another man's reputation over his damn pride. Luke wondered how much pride a man actually had when he was willing to do something low-down dirty like that.

It didn't matter. Seabrook was angry, and Luke doubted he'd let up soon. Which meant if Luke didn't get to Joanne and straighten this mess out in the next two weeks, he'd miss the Houston rodeo. Even second place offered a big enough purse that he'd have the money to put down on that sweet spread outside of San Antonio. With his savings, he'd buy horses and cattle. But only if his shoulder held out.

A damn big if.

The aroma of brewing coffee seeped into the

room, and he stopped rubbing his cock long enough to check the time again. Only five minutes had passed. But it was past time to get up. First a shower, and then he'd find his way to the kitchen for some of that coffee.

He swung his legs out of bed and, before his feet hit the floor, the ache started. Both shoulders, his lower back, his thighs. Too many fractures and broken bones. Thirty-three and he felt like he was seventy-three. But he couldn't quit yet. No matter what the doctors said.

HE LIMPED BADLY, probably should have been using a cane. From the kitchen window, Annie watched Chester, shoulders stooped and holding a pail in each hand, come from the barn toward the house. Her heart broke with every uneven step he took. He'd already looked old the last time she'd been here, and that had been a long time ago; there had always been something more important going on in her life than visiting her aging aunt.

Annie sniffed, and blinked a couple of times. She wasn't one to get emotional, but guilt had a way of obliterating her defenses. Looking away, she got out another mug and the small pitcher of cream Aunt Marjorie always kept in the refrigerator. Annie specifically remembered that Chester used cream. He'd always drank his coffee nearly white and sickeningly sweet.

After a brief knock at the door, Chester came in. He grinned wide, a lower tooth missing, which had been gone forever. "Hi, honey," he said, and put down the pails. "You're looking pretty as ever."

"And I see you still need glasses." She went into his open arms and hugged his thin body. He'd lost a lot of weight since she'd seen him last but, remarkably, his hair was still more red than gray. "It's good to see you, Chester."

He still smelled like fresh cut hay.

"Good to see you, too, missy. Been a long while."

"Yes, I know." Her face flushed. "Too long. Come sit and have a cup of coffee."

"Don't mind if I do." He limped across the aged yellow linoleum floor and removed his battered brown hat before sitting down at the table. "Not that I ain't happy to see you, but I told Marjorie she didn't need to call and bother you. It's not like Marjorie's any help when she's here."

Annie swallowed hard. "Has she been sick long?"

"What?" Chester's bushy eyebrows drew together. "Oh, I just meant that she's too busy being bossy to get any real work done."

"Ah. Well, that's good." Smiling to herself, she brought two mugs of coffee to the table.

"Ain't nothing good about it. How's a man supposed to get any peace and quiet while he's getting his chores done?"

"If you want peace and quiet, Chester, why aren't you retired?"

Snorting, he made a face. "That's for city folks." After dumping three large teaspoonfuls of sugar into his coffee, he took an appreciative sip. "Whose truck is that you're driving?"

She'd almost forgotten about the man down the hall. How that was possible was beyond her comprehension, since it had taken her over an hour to fall asleep last night, even though she was dead on her feet. "Do you know a Luke McCall?"

Chester's weathered face creased in a frown. "Luke? Yeah, I know the boy. Fritz McCall's grandson. Ain't seen him in a good long while. Why are you asking?"

"He's here." She tilted her head toward the bedrooms. "It's his truck."

Chester's mouth dropped open, his gaze went to the empty hallway. "Luke is here?"

She nodded. "I landed my rental car in a ditch last night. I was lucky he came along when he did."

"Luke is here," he repeated, his grin growing wider. "I'll be a monkey's uncle. Where is that son of a gun?"

"Still sleeping, I think."

Chester absently shook his head. A faraway look came into his watery blue eyes and his smile faded. "Wish he could've made it to his granddad's funeral. I figure he didn't come on account of his mother. Dang shame, though."

Annie was dying to know what Chester meant, but she kept her mouth shut because she didn't like anyone nosing around her personal business, either. She only smiled and sipped her coffee.

"He say why he's here?" Chester asked.

"He has some kind of business to tend to. Plus, he's between jobs."

Chester looked confused for a moment, and then let out a howl. "Between jobs, is he?"

"That's what he said." What was the big joke? The more he laughed, the more annoyed she became. "What am I missing here?"

"You old goat. Thought they'd put you out to pasture by now."

At the sound of Luke's voice, they both turned. His hair still damp, he wore jeans that rode low on his hips, no shirt, and a white towel draped around his neck.

Chester pushed up from the table with impressive ease and speed. "You come here and smart mouth me, boy."

The two men embraced, giving each other a quick hug, before standing back to eye each other. "You look good, you old coot," Luke said. "Mrs. W. seems to be taking good care of you."

Chester grunted. "The woman never could cook." He slid a sheepish look at Annie. "Beggin' your pardon, Annie."

She shrugged. "You're right. She cooks everything to mush."

Ironically, for years Annie thought her aunt was the greatest cook in the world. Easy assumption since the rest of the year she mostly ate peanut butter sandwiches because that was something a seven-year-old could make for herself. The real treat was when her father brought home fast food. Always cold because he'd inevitably stop at the racetrack on the way home, but at least it was something her daddy had brought her and she'd gobbled it down as if every bite was an expression of his love. Foolish child that she'd been.

Chester looked hopefully at Annie. "I don't suppose you know how to cook."

"Breakfast I can handle."

"I brought in fresh eggs," he said, indicating the pail he'd left at the door. "I know Marjorie always keeps ham steak and bacon in the ice box or the freezer."

"How about you?" she asked, looking at Luke, though trying really hard not to stare at his bare chest. With the sun streaming in through the kitchen window, his incredible blue eyes shone like sapphires. "Hungry?"

"I could eat." He gave her one of those heart-stopping grins that made her question the wisdom of having him stay here in the house. "I'll make toast."

"Okay, then after breakfast how about we go get my car?"

"Sure thing." He turned to Chester. "You have any strong rope we could use?"

"Yep. Out in the barn." He started to get up, but both Annie and Luke protested at the same time.

Luke put a hand on the man's shoulder. "We'll go out to the barn together after breakfast. How's that?"

The older man's expression turned indignant.

"I wanted to talk to you privately, anyway," Luke whispered.

"Gonna explain why you didn't come to your

granddaddy's funeral, I suppose." Chester settled back in his chair and took a sip of his coffee, his watchful eyes on Luke.

His face darkened. "Now, don't you start in on me, old timer."

"I ain't startin' in on you. I figure you had a reason and you might be wantin' to get it off your chest."

"You know why I couldn't come," Luke said, lowering his voice and sliding an exasperated glance at Annie.

Chester chuckled. "Couldn't or wouldn't?"

Annie quickly went back to the business of getting out the frying pan and plugging in the toaster. But it wasn't as if she could pretend she hadn't heard. She could at least pretend she wasn't curious as hell.

An awkward silence grew and then Luke said, "I'm gonna go put on a shirt, and then I'll help with breakfast."

She turned to watch him leave, already mourning the loss of all that glorious tanned skin and well-developed muscle. Out of the corner of her eye, she caught Chester watching her. "Do I have to do anything to the eggs?" she asked and when he frowned she added, "Before I cook them."

He laughed heartily. "Them are fresh eggs, missy. All you do is crack 'em and fry 'em."

"I knew that," she muttered, feeling sheepish and annoyed. "I talked to Aunt Marjorie this morning. She sounds in good spirits."

"I know. I talked to her an hour ago."

"Oh." Annie shouldn't have been surprised. "She told me the doctor said they should be done with her tests by Monday and then they'd release her."

"Now if that don't happen, don't you fret. Your aunt's an impatient woman."

She poured a little oil into the frying pan for the smoked ham she'd found in the refrigerator drawer. Taking a deep breath, she asked, "Is there anything I should know that Aunt Marjorie isn't telling me?"

He took a thoughtful sip of coffee, saying nothing for a long uncomfortable moment. "Don't believe I know what she told you."

"I'm a cop, Chester. I know when someone's evading me."

"Respectin' your aunt's privacy is all I'm doin'."

"Look, I know I haven't been around and have no right to ask to be involved but—"

"Hold up there, missy. I never said that. I don't feel that way neither." Sighing, he pushed a hand through his thinning hair, so uneven he had to have cut it himself. "She's been havin' faintin' spells lately."

"Okay." She put the ham in the pan to brown, and took her mug of coffee with her to the table so she could look Chester in the eyes. "And?"

"She won't eat right."

"You mean she's not eating."

His concerned expression got to her. "Your aunt, stubborn old mule that she is, won't admit she's got diabetes."

"What?" Annie set down her mug before she

dropped it. "But she's got packages of cookies in the cupboard and homemade fudge in the fridge and— for crying out loud, she's got more sweets in this house than anything else."

"Yep. She's got a sweet tooth all right."

"But she knows she can't have sugar, right? I mean, this is totally treatable."

"She knows."

"God, Chester." Annie's gaze jumped to the outdated, scarred cupboards. "Does she have a death wish or something?"

"Say what?"

Annie sighed heavily, staring at the uneven yellow linoleum. "Is it about money? This place needs so much— She sent me money, Chester. For tuition. For Christmas, for…"

She saw something move by the door. Luke stood there, about to enter the kitchen, the sympathetic look on his face more disturbing than if he'd accused her of being an uncaring selfish bitch.

"You listen here," Chester said, his back to Luke. "Your aunt wanted you to have that money. It was important to her that you had a good education. Especially after your mother ran off like that, and then your father—"

"Do I smell something burning?" Luke asked, effectively stopping Chester.

"Uh, thanks, the ham." Annie's eyes met his gaze as she rose from the table. The ham wasn't burning. He knew she was uncomfortable with him listening.

"I've got to make a phone call," he announced, "and my cell battery is dead. I'll be back in five minutes."

"Use that one." Chester pointed to the brown old-fashioned wall phone.

Annie saw the reluctance in Luke's face. Obviously, he wanted privacy and she didn't blame him. "There's one in Aunt Marjorie's bedroom. It'll be quieter in there."

"Thanks." His smile reached his eyes and warmed the feminine part of her that hadn't felt like that in a really long time.

"Breakfast will be ready in ten."

"I'll be back in time to make the toast."

She smiled. "Okay."

After he left, she glanced over at Chester. His mouth started to curve to match the amused twinkle in his eyes.

"What?" Her tone dared him to comment.

"Nothing, missy. Nothing at all." He brought the mug to his lips, but it barely hid his grin.

LUKE CLOSED THE bedroom door before picking up the receiver and dialing Joanne Seabrook's phone number. Five times it rang before a woman with a Spanish accent answered.

Two sisters worked for the Seabrook's, Yolanda and Margarita. One liked him and the other didn't. Not wanting to take a chance, he disguised his voice. "May I speak with Mrs. Seabrook, please?"

The woman hesitated. "May I tell her who's calling?"

"Simon from the spa, regarding her appointment tomorrow morning." Luke knew she had a weekly appointment at a spa near Fort Worth, but he couldn't recall the exact name.

"One moment, please."

He waited a long time before he heard the faint clicking of heels on a hardwood floor. Which meant she was answering the phone in the foyer. Damn. No privacy.

"Hello?" Her voice was soft with a hint of the south. He'd found it charming once. Until he'd found out she'd lied to him.

"Joanne?"

"Who is this?"

"Joanne, it's—"

A clattering sound cut him off. As if she'd dropped the phone.

"You son of a bitch." It was Seabrook, screaming into the phone like a lunatic. "You damn coward. Where are you? Get your ass back here or I'll have it dragged back."

Luke quietly hung up the phone.

"SON OF A BITCH hung up on me." Ernest Seabrook stuck the cigar in his mouth, his fat jowls working as he puffed on the smelly thing.

Joanne sighed, noticing that her red nail polish had chipped on her ring finger. "What did you expect? Yelling at him like some madman."

"Don't you sass me, woman." Ernest narrowed his

icy blue eyes and gave her that disapproving fatherly look she detested. At least he stopped puffing for a moment. "I haven't forgiven you yet. Don't rightly know that I ever will."

"Oh, Ernie." She slid an arm through his and urged him toward the French doors that led to the garden and swimming pool. "I told you that nothing happened. Why won't you believe me?"

Ernest scoffed. "He was here for two hours and nothing happened?"

"Who told you he was here that long?" She led him to the wrought iron loveseat near the bar and gently pushed him onto the blue striped cushions. He didn't resist, which meant she was home free.

"Never you mind."

"It was Yolanda, wasn't it?" Of course it was. The bitch. Yolanda thought she was too good to be a maid and that she should be Mrs. Ernest Seabrook. Ha! Ernie liked his women pale and blond. Joanne slid her palm up and down his beefy arm. "She lied. You know she doesn't like me. In fact, she hated me on sight."

She moved her hand from his arm to his upper thigh, and he made that disgusting moaning sound. Joanne forced a smile and then touched his lower lip with the tip of her tongue. "She didn't want you to marry me," she whispered. "This past year, she's been horrible to me. You don't hear the things she says."

"Now, don't fret. I'll have a talk with her." He opened her mouth with his horrid tongue and stuck it inside.

She did all she could not to shudder, and comforted herself by eyeing the three-carat diamond ring on her finger. The man had more money than most people even dreamed of. She knew where he kept some of the cash. The silver and gold bars he had buried somewhere on his property that extended over a thousand acres, so they were pretty much out of reach.

"It would make me really happy if you fired her." She cupped her hand over his cock and used just the right amount of pressure she knew he liked. Then she took it away.

He grabbed her wrist and squeezed painfully. "I know you screwed Luke McCall," he said in a low menacing voice. "Don't think I've forgotten." And then he forced her hand back over his cock and closed his evil eyes.

5

ANNIE FOLLOWED Luke back to the ranch in her rental car. It had been clean when she picked it up at the Dallas-Fort Worth airport yesterday evening. Now, mud splattered the bottom half and caked the wheel casings. The right side of the bumper had a small dent that Luke thought he could fix.

She hadn't paid attention to how they got back to the spot where her car was, but returning to the ranch seemed to take forever. Partly because he'd taken so many dirt roads instead of going through town.

As soon as they pulled up in front of the house, she got out and met him at his truck. He opened his door but didn't get out. Facing the sun, she had to shade her eyes to look at him. "Why the scenic tour?"

His mouth started to curve. "Nothing scenic about Morgan's Road or Duck Creek. Some time back it was a—"

"All right, all right. I don't need a local history lesson." She sighed, sorry she'd been short. But looking around at all the work that needed to be done depressed the hell out of her. In the daylight everything looked worse. Half the white picket fence was down and weeds were starting to overtake the two flower beds on either side of the porch.

"I wanted to go through town so I could pick up a couple of things. Now I'll have to go back." She tensed. He was staring at her. "What?"

"You have pretty eyes."

She snorted, embarrassed mostly. No one had ever told her that before. And she didn't believe it anyway. He was simply making conversation, the way charming, good-looking guys like Luke did with women.

"I like the way they change color." His gaze drifted to her mouth and then slowly rose to meet her eyes again.

She cleared her throat. "Are you getting out of the truck or not?"

"I'm putting it in the barn." He reached for the door handle and she stepped out of the way. "Chester cleared out a spot for me."

"Why?"

"I don't like nosy neighbors knowing I'm here."

"*Here* meaning at the ranch, or back in town?"

He smiled. "You gonna interrogate me, Sergeant?"

"The nearest neighbor has to be two miles away. So I have to assume you don't want anyone to know you're back."

"That assumption would be correct." He closed the door. "Is that all, Sarge?"

"Actually, I have a bunch of questions."

"Cranky when you don't get enough sleep, huh?" He grinned and put the truck in reverse. "Don't go to town yet. We're supposed to meet with Chester and go over which repairs to tackle."

"Right." She checked her watch. Mostly for something to do. Other than stare at him. He was just too damn pretty for her own good. "After that, I'll go get what we need. Maybe Chester will go with me, since you're hiding out."

He didn't take the bait. Just backed up enough to turn the truck toward the barn. Chester opened the rickety door for him, and after Luke parked, Chester closed it, having to pull and tug because the frame had warped. For Luke, Annie had a feeling Chester would do almost anything. Coconspirators was what they were.

After Luke had left to make his phone call earlier, she'd tried subtly to question Chester. All he'd say was that Luke rode the rodeo circuit and that was the joke about being between jobs. There was more to it, she was certain, but all she could do was trust Chester. Anyway, as long as Luke helped with the repairs, what did she care? In a week she'd be back in New York and she'd never see Luke McCall again.

"HAND ME THE pliers, will you?" Luke used the back of his arm to wipe the sweat from his forehead. He'd taken his hat off about an hour ago, letting the sun draw out the honey-colored streaks in his hair. "Annie? The pliers?"

"Oh, sorry." She kept hold of her side of the wire and stretched to hand them to him.

This was the second time she'd been too busy staring at the way his back muscles worked under the blue western shirt to hear him.

He twisted the barbed wire around the top of the new post he'd put in to fill a gap where the cows had been escaping. Fortunately, the south pasture was the only place they had to worry about, since Aunt Marjorie was down to four cows.

Damn good thing. The sun was blazing hot and the sky so clear there wasn't a cloud in sight to give them relief. Not to mention the bugs. Oh, God. The welts had started plumping up a half hour ago. On her legs, her arms, her back. No place was sacred to the miniature vampires. When they were done working, she was going right to town to get some spray.

"Can you stretch that about an inch more?" Luke asked. She grabbed the wire with both gloved hands and pulled as hard as she could. The wire stretched about half an inch.

She ran five miles six days a week and worked out at the gym three times a week, so she knew she was doing her share. It had nothing to do with vanity, but everything to do with maintaining her stamina so she could do her job. Every year the bad guys seemed to be getting younger and faster.

As fit as she was, mending fences and digging post holes was hard work. She was ready for a bath and a nap, but not until she got that wire stretched another half an inch. She braced her feet and leaned back, using all her weight.

Her right tennis shoe connected with a loose rock and she teetered for a moment. She tried to hold on to the fence but scraped her bare arm on the barbed wire. She jerked away, lost her balance and landed on her rear end in the tall, bug-infested grass.

She ground out a pithy curse that would've made her aunt blush.

Luke laughed. "You okay?"

She slapped at her leg. There might have been a bug crawling up, or else it was just the creepy-crawlies. But she wasn't taking any chances. "Your concern is touching."

He wrapped his side of the wire around a post and pulled off a glove as he walked over to her. "Here."

She eyed his extended hand and then let him pull her to her feet. The rocky ground made it difficult for her to gain her footing, but he held on to her until she stabilized herself. He shook his head at the bloody gash on her arm, taking her by the forearm and bringing it up for a closer look. It did seem pretty nasty, but she'd live.

"Hope you've had a tetanus shot recently." He hadn't released her, and if she were in any danger at all, it was from his nearness. Or maybe it was the heat making her lightheaded.

"I'm good. Two years ago." The day she'd inter-rupted a store robbery and the crackhead sliced her left thigh. She tried to move away from Luke, but apparently he wasn't through with her.

He pulled a red bandana out of his back pocket, inspected it to make sure it was clean and then, from the canteen he'd brought, poured some water on the cloth.

She waved a dismissive hand. "It'll be fine until I get back to the house."

"Let's at least get it clean."

"Look, I— Ouch!" She tried to pull back her arm but he wouldn't let go.

"Hold still."

She closed her eyes, surprised at how much it stung. When she looked at the wound, it was deeper and uglier than she'd thought.

"Tell me if you think you're gonna faint."

She looked up at him, saw that he was serious and laughed. "I've been held at gunpoint twice, shot once and stabbed. Trust me, I'm not going to faint."

His eyes narrowed to a squint. "You're serious."

"Damn straight."

"Where did you get shot?"

"At a liquor store."

He gave her a wry look.

Annie smiled. "Right here," she said and pulled the neckline of her T-shirt to expose her shoulder. "Actually, I was lucky, the bullet only grazed me." Still, the sucker had left an ugly scar. She had no idea why she was showing it to Luke. She pulled her neckline back in place.

Luke put his hand over hers, and then gently

pushed the shirt back again and stared in disbelief at the elongated scar.

His silence said it all. She covered the scar again, and this time he didn't stop her. "Hazards of the job."

"What happened?"

"I was a beat cop on patrol, practically a rookie. My partner and I walked past an alley where a drug deal was going down. We heard a commotion. We had no idea what was happening until they pulled out their guns. A couple of shots and then they ran. Lucky for us."

"Lucky?"

"Well, yeah, considering we were unprepared."

"So they got away?"

She snorted. "Yeah."

"Too bad."

She shrugged. "It happens."

"Here." He passed her the canteen, a smile lifting his lips. "You earned a drink."

She took it. "Oh, I have to get gouged to earn a drink?"

"Naw, you get whatever you want just for coming out here to help."

"What? Why wouldn't I?"

He briefly touched a lock of hair that had escaped her ponytail. "I shouldn't have let you."

"Let me?"

"You know what I mean. This is hard work and most women really aren't strong enough to— Hey, what are you doing?"

Annie swung him around and brought his arm up

behind him. He tried to break away but she pulled his arm up higher until he groaned. "You were saying, Mr. McCall?"

"Listen, don't take it personally."

She gave another tug.

"All right, let me go."

"Take back what you said." She leaned into him to give herself more leverage, but her breasts pressing against his back didn't help her concentrate.

"I don't wanna hurt you, Annie."

"Give it your best shot."

"Come on, now."

She tightened her hold on his arm.

"Okay, but I warned you." He'd barely finished speaking when he broke away, grunting when his arm twisted with the struggle.

Suddenly, he was facing her, grinning. "Now, what do you have to say?"

She caught him by surprise, landing a well-placed kick right above his groin. Not hard, just enough to shock him. "I say you need to practice more."

He stepped back, away from her lethal tennis shoe, just in case. "You could've really hurt me, darlin'."

"'Could have' being the operative words. However, I not only have strength and cunning, but I have great aim—and restraint." She smiled sweetly.

"Where did you learn that?"

"Kickboxing every Tuesday and Thursday, baby."

Laughing, he stretched and scratched his chest in a way that was typically male.

The distraction threw her off her guard. In an instant, he had her wrapped in his arms. She brought up her knee, not really intending to use it, but he looped an arm underneath her thigh and the next thing she knew she was flat on her back in the grass, with one particularly long blade tickling her ear.

"You okay?" he had the nerve to ask, holding one of her wrists and sprawling over her, though not quite touching, which was almost worse.

"Fine." Like hell. She couldn't breathe. Had he lowered his head or was that her imagination? "Are you going to get off now?"

"I'll have to think about that one." His eyes were so dilated they almost looked black. "Am I hurting you?"

"No." Her voice was barely a whisper.

"Good." He brushed his lips across hers, and then touched the corners of her mouth with his tongue, tasting, testing.

"All right," she said, embarrassed at her husky whisper. "Round one goes to you."

Luke smiled. "Not yet."

Her heart lurched. She lifted her head slightly, and he accepted the invitation by lowering his body so that his chest grazed her hardened nipples. He shifted so that one of his thighs laid over hers, pressing her intimately. She wanted to squeeze her legs together to stop the burn that was slowly building. Instead, she just lay there, holding her breath, until it came out in a warm shuddering rush across his chin.

He shifted again, and this time she felt the thick

bulge behind his fly. The air was hot and sticky but she didn't care. She wanted to take more of his weight. She wanted to rip his shirt off and feel his bare chest against her bare breasts.

"I've been wanting to kiss you since last night," he said softly, pushing her hair away from her face and pressing his lips to her jaw.

"We only met last night."

"Is that a problem?"

Annie smiled. Not for her.

He leaned back and pulled the remaining glove off his left hand. The implication alone sent a shiver through her and she moved to disguise it, bringing them in more intimate contact. She heard his sharp intake of breath and felt his hardness rub her thigh.

Someone cleared their throat.

Luke looked up first. She followed his gaze.

Chester stood there, his face redder than his hair. Averting his eyes, he said, "Beggin' your pardon, Luke. It looks like we might have a problem."

"SON OF A BITCH," Luke muttered, stopping abruptly outside the barn as he watched Billy McIntosh snoop through the back of the truck.

"Dang it. I told him to stay away from there. He's just supposed to feed the chickens and round up the cows and then go home. Sorry, I forgot to tell you about him. Marjorie insisted I needed help. Damn stubborn woman." Chester started inside but Luke stopped him.

Annie growled in frustration. "Would somebody please tell me what's going on?"

Her raised voice made Billy look up. The twelve-year-old broke into a wide grin. "I knew it was you." He rushed up to Luke. "My friends aren't gonna believe this. Can I see your buckles, Mr. McCall?"

"Hold on there, son." Luke removed his Stetson hat to mop his forehead. His hair and shirt stuck to him. And, damn if he wasn't still a little hard. He was hot and horny, and now he had to worry about this kid shooting his mouth off around town. "What makes you think I'm McCall?"

"I saw you ride last summer. The San Antonio rodeo. My folks took me for my birthday." His wide grin showed off a wide gap between his two front teeth. The kid looked familiar, but the only reason Luke knew his name was because Chester told him.

"Well, son, sorry to tell you that you're mistaken." He knew Annie was staring. He ignored her. He hoped the kid did, too. "I do ride rodeo, though. You just have me and Luke mixed up."

Billy's face puckered into a surly frown. "No, I don't. I saw you up close when you signed my autograph. Plus, my mom has a picture of you when you were young. Says she went out with you in high school." He sniffed and ran his arm under his nose. "Makes my dad madder than a hornet that she keeps your picture in her drawer."

Luke glanced at Chester, who suddenly seemed to find something interesting up on the ceiling. Luke turned his attention back to the boy. "What's your mama's name?"

"Sally Jo McIntosh."

Shit. There was only one Sally Jo. Hawkins was her last name back in high school, and she was the pushiest girl he'd ever made out with. Even later, when he'd come back to town and she'd already been married for three years, she'd been in his face. Baby in her arms and all.

He looked closer at Billy. This was probably him. The kid who'd only been about one at the time. Brother, if this didn't make him feel like a damn old man.

"Okay, look, Billy, this is the deal," Luke said, taking him off to the side, trying to make him feel important and trustworthy. "Can you keep a secret?"

His brown eyes widened. "Sure."

"You gotta promise."

"Cross my heart," he said, making the appropriate *X* across his narrow chest.

Luke slid a look at Annie. Her arms were folded, impatience written all over her face. There were gonna be more questions, dammit. "This is the thing, Billy. I came to town to surprise someone, so I can't let anyone know I'm here or it would ruin the surprise. You understand?"

The boy nodded, his eyes lighting up. "Who you gonna surprise?"

"I can't tell you that."

Billy's expression fell. "But I promised I could keep a secret."

"Doesn't matter. You don't know her."

Billy didn't look as if he wanted to cooperate. "When can I tell everyone?"

"About a week."

That wasn't gonna fly, judging by the frown wrinkling the boy's freckled nose.

"Maybe sooner. Look, how about I give you three free tickets to the Houston rodeo and an auto-graphed poster?"

"I got a baby brother."

"Okay, four tickets."

Billy grinned. "Deal."

Luke shook his hand. "Okay, buddy…" Too pain-ful to call him son anymore. It had been okay—until Luke was reminded how old he was. "Don't forget. You can't tell anyone. Not even your best friend."

Billy made a motion as though he was zipping his lips.

"Good man." Luke clapped the boy on his bony shoulder.

"See you tomorrow, Mr. McCall."

"Tomorrow?"

"Yeah, when I come feed the chickens and stuff." He'd started walking backward, and then turned and ran like hell toward the road. Probably couldn't wait to tell the whole damn town.

6

AS SOON AS BILLY left, Chester disappeared, too. Annie wondered if it was because he expected questions from her. He would've been right. Boy, did she have questions. Autographs? Buckles? Sally Jo?

She watched Luke walk around to the back of his truck and immediately her gaze fell to the snug fit of his jeans, to the way the denim molded his perfect ass. Her heart actually flip-flopped. Then she thought about what they'd been doing in the grass and how Chester had caught them, and her face flamed. She'd felt him— his chest, his thighs. His lips. God, she hoped it hadn't been a mistake. She hoped they'd do it again.

It took her a moment to realize he was rifling through the few belongings he'd brought with him. Did he think the kid had stolen something? Or was he simply avoiding her? Probably the latter. Not that it mattered.

She waited as patiently as she could until he started toward her, a grim look on his face. "What's going on?" she asked, when it appeared that he'd likely walk right by her if she didn't stop him.

"Nothing."

"So did you lie to that kid, or are you lying to me?"

He passed a weary hand over his face and sighed.

"Don't tell me it's none of my business, either, because you're staying in my aunt's house, with me, and if you're in some kind of trouble—"

"No, nothing like that." He looked away, which didn't exactly reassure her. "Look, I know his mama, okay? And I don't particularly want to see her."

Annie didn't buy it. Not when he had such trouble looking her in the eyes. "You didn't seem to know who his mother was, until he told you."

"You wanted me to admit to the kid that it was his mama I'm hiding from? That wouldn't be very kind, would it?" He started walking toward the house, and Annie stayed alongside him.

"Is she an old girlfriend?" Okay, now she was being nosy.

"Not exactly."

"That doesn't tell me anything."

He stopped and faced her. "How is this relevant?"

The sun hit her square in the face, so she had to squint to see him. His hat shaded his eyes. "Never mind. Forget it. But, if you bring any trouble here, you're gone."

He blinked, slowly exhaling. "Sally Jo and I went out once when we were kids. She got a little obsessive, and being married hasn't seemed to change that. The last time I saw her, the way she acted was downright shameful for a married woman. I'm trying to avoid trouble, not bring it on."

God help her if she was being a fool, but he looked so sincere. "I respect that," she said quietly. "In fact I admire your integrity. There's no reason anyone needs to know you're here."

"I'll admit, I've had my share of women. But never married ones." Disgust flashed across his face, and then he blinked and shook his head. "I'm gonna grab a shower and get something to eat. Wanna join me?"

Annie pressed her lips together. "In the shower or to have something to eat?"

A slow smile curved his mouth. "Well, now, that's an interesting question."

"I was kidding." Like hell she was. If circumstances were different, she'd be signing up for more. Maybe tonight, after they finished working. Texas was a couple thousand miles away from New York. Sex here wouldn't count.

His eyes darkened with a predatory interest and his fingers flexed. "I wouldn't mind the company."

Truly, she was tempted. "Shouldn't we get the fence finished?"

He nodded slowly, as if he'd forgotten. "Right." Then he checked his watch. "I have to make a phone call first. Why don't you go get something cold to drink and I'll meet you in the kitchen?"

"Okay," she said, but he hadn't even waited for her response. He was already heading for the house.

It wasn't in her nature to be this nosy. So why did she want to know who he was calling?

DAMN. YOLANDA ANSWERED.

"May I please speak to Margarita?" Luke figured he'd use a different tactic and a pronounced southern accent. Margarita liked him. She might get Joanne to the phone without giving him up to Seabrook.

"May I tell her who is calling?"

Man. What a witch. "Fred."

"Is she expecting your call?"

He could tell by her tone that she suspected it was him. But she couldn't be sure, so just maybe... "I believe she is, darlin'."

"One moment, please, señor."

While he waited, half expecting Seabrook to bark in his ear, he glanced around Mrs. W's bedroom. Annie was sleeping in this room since he had the only available spare room. Like the rest of the house, its rugs and curtains were worn and faded. The massive oak four-poster and dresser had to have been passed down a few generations and were likely considered expensive antiques.

What grabbed his attention was Annie's open suitcase. She was obviously one of those really neat ones, everything folded so precisely that it made you not wanna disturb it. The stack was so perfect; how could she find anything? You'd have to take the whole thing apart just to see what was underneath.

Not him. One look in his bag and he knew everything that was in there.

"Hello?" Her voice in his ear startled him.

"Joanne?"

She laughed in that throaty way he used to find sexy. "I thought it might be you, lover. Margarita has never gotten a call here in her life."

"Is Seabrook there?"

"No, but he's due back at any moment."

"He thinks I stole the money."

"I know."

"But you can prove otherwise. I was never alone in the house. You were always with me. You gotta tell the sheriff this is about the old man's pride. There's no missing money. He's just trying to punish me. We both know that."

"Want to know what I'm wearing, sugar?" she whispered huskily.

"Joanne, this is serious. If that money is missing, he took it and he's trying to frame me." The dismal thought just occurred to him. He wouldn't put it past the slimy bastard to pocket the money and send him to prison.

"You know I'd help you if I could, but I swore to him that nothing happened between us. I can't very well admit you were here more than once, now can I?"

Luke exhaled slowly. How had he been so foolish? He was too old to be thinking with his dick. All this woman cared about was her meal ticket. She lied to Luke about who she was. No telling what she told Seabrook. "Why exactly did you tell him I was there?"

"I think he's home."

"Don't hang up, Joanne. Where can we meet?"

"I don't think that would be wise. But we can

have some fun over the phone. Ever have phone sex, lover?"

"Won't be able to do that from prison, will I, darlin'?"

"I heard the garage door. I've got to go."

"Wait. Can you get away tomorrow?"

She hesitated so long that he thought she'd hung up. "Give me your number."

"You have my cell number."

"Where are you?"

"At a friend's place." Luke wasn't that stupid. He didn't trust her. Might give him up to Seabrook to make sure her monthly allowance kept rolling in.

"Here in Valley View?"

"No."

Her throaty laugh grated on him. "Sounds like you don't trust me, sugar. I hope I'm wrong."

"Of course I trust you." He smiled. "I trust you to do the right thing and come forth on my behalf."

"He's coming," she said, and hung up.

Luke cursed and slammed down the receiver, then checked to make sure he hadn't cracked the phone. Joanne wasn't going to tell the truth. She had a prenuptial agreement and she wasn't willing to risk losing the lavish lifestyle.

If he could tape record their conversation... He sat on the edge of the bed, trying to think about his next move. It seemed that, if he wanted a meeting, he'd have to surprise her someplace public. The only place he knew for sure where she'd be was at that spa—six days from now.

He scanned the room for a calendar. He found something far more interesting. On a hook on the back of the door hung a black lacy teddy. He smiled, picturing Annie wearing it and showing off her long slim legs. Sergeant Corrigan was an interesting woman.

"COME AND HAVE A glass of lemonade with me, Chester," Annie called from the kitchen door. She didn't feel guilty for inviting the old man to sit with her, even though she fully intended to pump him for information—subtly of course. He never took a break, always kept working. Someone had to get him to slow down. "In fact, how about I fix you some lunch?"

"Don't go to no trouble, missy." He'd started walking toward her from the barn. "A tall glass of cold lemonade would be fine. Can't say that I've had any for quite a spell."

"Good." She smiled and went back inside to take out the deli ham and cheese. While she got out the bread and mayonnaise, through the kitchen window she watched him limp slowly toward the house.

A lump lodged in her throat. How could he and Aunt Marjorie continue to maintain the place? Not that it was maintained now. With only one week, she and Luke could hardly make a dent in all the needed repairs.

She'd have to talk to her aunt about moving into a small apartment in one of those assisted living places. Annie could help pay for it. Even if she had to quit going to evening classes. The small savings she'd acquired would help, too. It wasn't as if she'd ever be able to afford her own place in New York.

She heard Chester's perfunctory knock, and then he came into the kitchen. He took off his hat, gave her a brief smile, yet looked away as he pulled out a chair and slowly lowered himself. When he still didn't look up, she got it. Her. Luke. Rolling in the grass. Okay, so they weren't rolling. That was the problem.

"Here you go." She set the frosty glass of lemonade on the table. "I'm making sandwiches, too."

"Told you not to go to no trouble."

"Then you'll be happy to know it's no trouble at all."

"You got a lot of your aunt Marjorie in you."

She smiled back and returned to the business of sandwich making, wondering how she was going to broach the subject and set the record straight. "We're having ham and cheese. Mustard or mayo?"

"Since you're askin', I wouldn't mind a little of each."

"You got it." So was it better to talk sitting across from him so she could see his expression, or while she was busy at the counter?

"Where's Luke?"

"Making a phone call."

He chuckled. "That boy sure does like the phone."

"Yeah." She grinned. "Chester, about earlier…"

He put up a hand. "None of my business."

"I know. But it really wasn't what it looked like. "I'd fallen backward and Luke was helping me up and—" The explanation sounded lame, even to her. "Would you like a pickle with your sandwich?"

"No, thanks."

"We have cookies for later, too."

"I didn't smell any baking."

"Um, they're packaged cookies I picked up at the grocery store."

"Cookies come in packages now?"

She abruptly turned around.

He looked serious at first and then winked. "You remember your aunt's sugar cookies? Makes my mouth water just thinking about 'em."

"No arguments here, they were the best." She cut his sandwich in half, then brought the plate to the table. "She'd always have a batch made when I'd come for the summer. I'd eat them 'till I was sick."

"She hasn't made any for a while, or if she has, she ain't told me because I get on her for eatin' 'em."

Annie brought the pitcher of lemonade to the table, sat down and refilled both their glasses. As much as she wanted to help get the place in better shape, maybe she should be in Houston with Aunt Marjorie. Maybe her aunt didn't understand the seriousness of her disease. Annie could talk to the doctors for her and interpret what they had to say.

"Hey, what are you getting so hang-dog for? Marjorie is gonna be all right. She's too ornery to let anything happen." He patted Annie's hand. "Where's your sandwich?"

"I'm not hungry. I think it's the heat." She fished

an ice cube out of her glass and ran it over her neck. "Those window air-conditioning units don't work very well. How old are they?"

Chester chewed thoughtfully. "Can't recall. Long time, though."

"I'll talk to Luke about replacing the ones in the bedroom and kitchen." Annie figured that was about all she could afford after buying more fencing and wood and paint.

"Doubt Luke will have the time. Besides, he'd have to go clear to Dallas to buy something like that."

"What do you mean Luke won't have time? He said he'd be around for days."

He shrugged and took another bite of his sandwich. "Maybe."

This was her opening. "Is there something I should know about him?"

"Nah, it's just that Luke—" He looked pensively out the window for a moment as if measuring his words. "He can't stay here in Hasting's Corner for long. He gets too fidgety. Too many bad memories, I reckon." He looked at her suddenly. "I'm not one for gossip."

"We're not gossiping. I have to be sure I can count on him."

"Worried I'm gonna renege on you?" Luke's voice came from the hallway.

She looked up as he entered the kitchen, a smirk on his face. His hair was damp and he had on a clean shirt. He hadn't shaved yet, and the memory of his

chin's abrasiveness on her skin made her chest tight-
en. "Actually, yes."

"Now why would you think that?"

Chester didn't look happy. He pushed his plate
away and stared straight ahead, probably beating
himself up for talking about Luke.

"Because I think you're distracted," Annie said
quickly. "I have a feeling that, as soon as you get
whatever problem you have solved, you'll take off."

He strolled past her to the counter where she'd left
out the sandwich stuff. "That a fact?"

She twisted around to look at him, wishing she'd
taken time for a shower. "Am I wrong?"

"Did I, or did I not, give you my word?" He got a
beer out of the fridge and opened it, before starting
to make his sandwich.

"Well, thanks for lunch and the lemonade." Chester pushed back from the table. "I still got me some
chores to do."

"Wait, Chester, I wanted to talk to both of you
about something."

"Sorry, the cows can't wait." Wincing as he got to
his feet, he carried his plate and glass to the sink.

"Why don't you wait up and I'll give you a hand?"

"Thank you kindly, but I've been doing it myself
for near sixty years." He scooped up his hat and
hobbled out the back door.

Annie shook her head, watching him slowly take
the two steps down. "He shouldn't still be working.
Neither of them should."

"What else would you expect them to do? Sit around and watch soap operas?"

She looked sharply at Luke. "They're both too old to handle this place, and you can't tell me otherwise."

He took a long pull of beer. "I agree, but that's not gonna stop them."

"Of course it won't. Not if they stay here. There will always be something to do."

Frowning at her, he carried his sandwich and beer to the table. "What are you saying?"

She took a sip of her lemonade and then licked the stickiness from the corners of her mouth. His fascinated interest was like a blast of heat. She pulled the neckline of her T-shirt away from her skin. It didn't do a thing to cool her off, especially when Luke's gaze slid lower and then lingered on her breasts.

"I'm going to talk to my aunt about selling the ranch."

He looked up to meet her eyes. "You're joking."

"It would be the sensible thing to do."

"And what about Chester?"

"He'd go with her."

Amusement lit his eyes as he brought his sandwich to his lips. "Go where?"

"I'm sure Dallas has a nice assortment of assisted-living communities."

Without taking a bite, he put his sandwich back down. "What the hell is that?"

"Well, it's pretty nice actually. Everyone has their

own apartment, but they eat together in a huge dining—"

"Apartment?"

She nodded. "Some of them are pretty roomy. Bigger than where I live."

"You're crazy, you know that?"

"What?"

"You might as well put that gun of yours to their heads and pull the trigger."

Annie stared at him dumbfounded. "That was a really, really horrible thing to say."

"These folks don't know any other kind of life. It would kill them to be dragged away."

"For God's sake, I'm not dragging them. They probably don't understand their options. We can do sufficient cosmetic repairs to make it attractive enough to sell. That would help with their monthly expenses. I could—" She looked at the calendar on her watch. Maybe she could still take the detectives exam. It would mean more money. Tomorrow morning she'd call the precinct first thing, see if she could fax a submission.

Yet, the thought of learning a new job gave her the willies. She was comfortable with the way things were. She liked being a sergeant. She was good at it, too. What if she turned out to be a lousy detective? Change sucked. She heard Luke snort and she looked over at him.

Shaking his head, he chewed a bite of his sandwich. "Glad you didn't bring it up with Chester. At least not while I was around."

She leaned back in her chair, immediately full of misgiving. And, to her shame, some relief, because maybe this wasn't something she could fix or should become involved with. Although Luke hadn't been around for a long time. What did he know about these people? She sighed. Probably a lot more than she did. But would she be doing what was in Aunt Marjorie's best interest if she didn't at least try to get her aunt into a more suitable place?

"I'm her only relative. I can't stay here and look after her and Chester. I would if I could. I have a job, a life back in New York. Well, sort of a life." Groaning softly, she folded her arms on the table, closed her eyes and laid her forehead on her forearms. All this thinking had given her a major headache. Or maybe it was the guilt for being so self-absorbed and blind that made her head hurt.

Annie hadn't even heard him get up. But she suddenly felt his large hands on her shoulders, kneading and rubbing, melting away the tension. She didn't even try to lift her head.

"Good. Just relax," he whispered.

Not a problem—she couldn't move. "Luke, what did you do about your grandfather?"

His hands stilled, and then fell away.

She lifted her head then and saw him leaving the kitchen.

7

THAT WAS A WOMAN FOR YOU. Couldn't just enjoy the moment. Had to go and kick up old news. Ask messy questions. Want to know your life history.

Luke grabbed a hammer and a sack of nails off a rack Chester had installed behind the barn door. At the same time, Luke made a mental note to pick up some two-by-fours and sandpaper when he went to buy the paint for the front porch. He had one hell of a lot of work to do before he pulled out of here. And damned if he'd leave one minute before he got everything done that he said he would.

"What can I do?" Annie quietly came up behind him.

There she was, getting in his way again. Grudgingly, he turned around. She'd obviously taken a shower; her face was scrubbed clean and her hair was pulled back in a fresh ponytail. And she was wearing shorts. Jeans that had been cut off. They weren't frayed yet and one leg looked slightly shorter than the other one.

She shifted her weight from one shapely leg to the

other. "It was just too hot. I couldn't stand it. They had a hole in them anyway."

He didn't make any pretense of checking out her legs. Long and perfectly muscled, like those lady track runners he saw on TV. "Nothing's gonna be open around here tomorrow. Sunday the whole town closes."

"All day?"

"Yep. After church everyone's got to go home and gossip about who showed up and who didn't and if anyone happened to be wearing a new dress."

"Rather cynical, aren't you?"

"It's the truth. Ask Chester." He sifted through a discarded pile of short planks to see if any were worth salvaging for repairing the front steps. He found one and handed it to her while he continued searching.

"Look, Luke, about what I said earlier—"

"No need to bring it up again."

"That question had nothing to do with you and everything to do with me. I feel guilty. I want to make it right for my aunt. And Chester, too."

He stopped and looked at her, when he heard the slight quiver in her voice.

She turned away, her shoulders sagging. "I grew up without a mother and hardly saw my father. Aunt Marjorie was very good to me. She even made sure I could go to college."

"Yeah."

She turned back and gave him a funny look. "She paid my tuition. She's needed all these repairs for who knows how long, but she sent money to me, instead."

He put down the board he'd been inspecting. "No reason for you to feel guilty. She's your aunt. She loves you. She chose to do that. That's what responsible, loving adults do. They protect their children. Just like it should be." Even he could hear the bitterness in his voice. He cleared his throat and started rummaging again.

"Thank you."

"For what?"

She came up behind him and put a hand on his arm. "For trying to make me feel better."

"Did it work?"

She smiled. "Let's get back to work before I collapse on the couch instead."

"Hmm. Couch. Horizontal. Sounds good."

Annie good-naturedly punched his arm. It was a light touch, but she got him just right, and pain shot all the way to his shoulder blade. He bit his lip to stop from crying out, but she saw it in his face.

Her eyes widened. "I am so sorry. I didn't think I punched you that hard."

"You didn't." He opened and closed his fist. It didn't help. Made the pain worse. He took a deep breath. "It's a pinched nerve or something."

"Can I get you anything?"

"No, it's getting better already."

"Liar."

He grabbed her by the wrist and pulled her close. "See?"

"If Chester walks in on us right now I'll die."

Luke chuckled. His arm still tingled but it was worth it to have her this close, when all he needed to do was lower his head and touch those pretty pink lips. He tilted her chin up. "You're still fretting about that?"

"I was a kid the last time I saw him."

"You aren't now."

"No," she whispered. "But—"

"Chester went to town," he said, and kissed her.

She kissed him back, pressing so close he could feel the hardness of her nipples through his T-shirt. He slid his arms around her and cupped her bottom and then felt a twinge in his shoulder. He tried to hide his discomfort, but he must have tensed because she went rigid.

She moved back to look at him. "Maybe you should go see a doctor."

"Hell, I've seen doctors." He stretched his neck to the side which seemed to help the top of his shoulder. "I'm sick of them."

"Can't they help you?"

He had to stop himself from biting her head off. She seemed genuinely concerned, and it wasn't her fault that he'd broken one too many bones. That every doctor he'd seen had told him to quit riding.

Shit. All he knew was bull riding. He was good at it. He knew he had to quit eventually, and then he'd try his hand at ranching. If he failed at that...

Annie was staring curiously at him, and he turned back to fishing out the planks he needed. "It's gonna take time to mend. That's all. I got painkillers but I'm not fond of taking them."

"Is that why you're *between jobs?*"

"Yep. Anyway, there's no competitions I'm interested in right now. Now, the Houston rodeo…that's big money. I'm not missing that one."

"When is it?"

"Next month."

She gasped. "Will you be healed by then?"

"For Pete's sake. How many questions are you gonna ask?"

She stared at him, looking even more curious, but said nothing.

He grabbed a coil of rope, looped it around his good shoulder and headed out of the barn. Wasn't that just like a woman? Asking too damn many questions. How was a man supposed to get any peace and quiet? Or, for one moment, forget his fears?

"HE'S CALLED HERE twice and you still can't find him." As usual Seabrook sounded out of breath, more than likely from smoking those nasty cigars. Wouldn't hurt him to lose seventy pounds, either.

"It's only been two days, Mr. Seabrook. We'll find him." Knowing what was to come, Jethro promptly held the phone away from his ear.

Seabrook let out a stream of curses that would make a drunk blush. "I need you to find him now! Have you got that, son? Am I making myself clear?"

"Yes, sir." Jethro calmly sipped the strong black

coffee the motel offered for free and let the man rant. He'd been a fool not to negotiate paid expenses with Seabrook. He wondered what the old buzzard would do if he turned in his motel and meal receipts.

"Are you listening to me, Jethro?"

"Yes, sir."

"I want you to call me every hour, and if—" He started coughing, a deep, hacking, violent cough that rattled in Jethro's ear.

"You all right, sir?"

More coughing and choking.

"Sheriff?" It was Joanne.

"Yes, ma'am." He straightened as if she could see him through the phone. Just the sound of her sweet voice got his cock's attention.

"Please call me Joanne." In the background, Seabrook continued to hack.

"Yes, ma'am."

She giggled, the lilting sound music to his ears. "Obviously, Ernie can't talk right now."

"Is he okay?"

"He'll be fine. Just a minute please." She pulled away from the phone but he could still hear her yell, "Ernie, would you at least walk away. How am I supposed to hear with you making all that noise?"

Ah, the loving wife. Jethro chuckled to himself. "I don't know that there's much more to say. He's got me working on a job but—"

She sighed, and he could picture her twisting her long silky-looking blond hair between her glossy red-tipped fingers. "I know. It's silly, really. Do you know Luke? He wouldn't steal any money. I'm sure he has enough of his own, anyway."

"Well, someone stole it, ma—, uh, Joanne," he said and, when she didn't respond, he asked, "How well do you know Luke McCall?"

She gasped. "Sheriff Wilcox, you explain to me what that's supposed to mean."

"Nothing, ma'am," he said quickly, having found out what he needed to know. She'd been boinking McCall, all right. Jethro had been in law enforcement long enough to gauge her reaction. "I was merely wondering as to the nature of his character, is all."

"I don't know him *that* well. I've only talked with him from time to time, like congratulating him after he's won a competition or saying hello when he's come to the house."

"Oh, that's another thing I wanted to ask. I thought there was bad blood between McCall and Mr. Sea-brook. What did Luke come to the house for?"

After a long awkward silence, she said, "I'm not sure. To see Ernest, I suppose."

Jethro smiled at her huffy tone. "But you person-ally don't think he took the money."

She hesitated. "I suppose he could have, but there were an awful lot of people here that week. In fact, we had a large dinner party. I imagine it could have been any one of our guests. Although none of our friends are criminals, absolutely not."

Very interesting. Seabrook had claimed there were

no other possibilities. Jethro reached for the pen and small pad he kept in his breast pocket and then remembered he hadn't pulled on a shirt yet. He'd slept in after staying up late to see if McCall would show up at his grandfather's ranch. "Can you give me the names of the people who'd been to your home in the last week?"

"Didn't my husband do that?"

"I believe he was about to, when he was overcome by that coughing fit." Yeah, right. That old man was obviously hiding something.

"Well, Sheriff, I leave these things to my husband. I'm sure he has your phone number."

"Yes, ma'am."

"Oh, and Sheriff, where are you?"

"In a motel outside of Hasting's Corner." Frowning, he swung his feet up on the lumpy mattress and laid back against the two pillows he'd stacked together. "Why?"

"When you get back to town, stop by and have tea with me." She lowered her voice to a husky tone that he knew she normally used when she was manipulating Seabrook. "Or maybe you'd like something stronger."

Jethro nearly dropped the receiver. He wasn't sure what to say. Seabrook was a means to an end. That was obvious because she was too hot and he was too old and fat for her to be with him. Jethro figured she was probably playing him right now. But that breathy voice made him think of those big, round, bouncing breasts of hers. And soon he was thinking with his dick like he had when he was sixteen.

"Jethro?"

He cleared his throat. "That's a mighty nice offer."

"Ernest isn't home in the afternoons. Call me, you hear?"

"I'll do that." A growing silence told him she'd hung up. He flipped his phone closed, laid his head back on the pillows and tried to concentrate on why she was trying to manipulate him. How was she involved? Did she want Luke to skate, because finding him would expose their affair?

Shit!

His hand had gone to his cock and his ability to reason disappeared. All he could think about were those big, round, bouncing breasts.

ANNIE HADN'T BEEN to Hasting's Corner since she'd been a kid. Back in Brooklyn she hadn't thought much about the little Texas town, yet her memories of the place were startlingly clear.

She parked her rental car in front of the market—a family owned concern called Mike's. Hers was the only sedan in the lot. This was cowboy country, so instead of horses at the hitching post, there were trucks. Lots of trucks. Really big ones with names like Turbo and Hemi, and while they might be used in place of the four-legged creatures of the Old West, they weren't loved any less. The gleam from the chrome alone could probably be seen in outer space, winking at the stars.

She remembered the trucks from her visits to Aunt Marjorie, and to a young girl, they seemed huge. Oddly, they still seemed large. And ridiculously clean, considering how many dirt roads were still being used by the locals. However, back then, there hadn't been apartments just off Main Street, or a candle shop, but the feel of the town was the same. Friendly. Casual. Like home.

Inside, Mike's hadn't changed much, either. There was nothing too fancy sold here. Just good food, lots of fresh beef and chickens, vegetables. The scent of freshly baked bread laced with cinnamon made her stomach growl and, although she knew she shouldn't, she headed for the bakery first.

She'd actually come here to get something for dinner. Something easy to cook in fact, since she tended to eat sandwiches and salads at home. But Luke and Chester had been working hard and she doubted mixed greens would do the trick.

There was a real nice-looking apple pie that she put in the cart. Next, she picked up French vanilla ice cream. And now that the truly important decision had been made, she got a large bake and serve lasagna, rolls still hot from the oven and more cold cuts for tomorrow's lunch.

That was enough. However, she couldn't help herself—she went through the store aisle by aisle. Her step slowed as she passed the spices, the pancake mixes, the canning supplies. It wasn't the particular items that held her rapt, but the calm, which wrapped her like a blanket.

Back home, her grocery store was a corner market perpetually crowded with commuters. No one chatted, not unless they wanted to complain. No one even smiled. Everyone knew everyone here, and they talked and laughed with the kind of ease she hardly ever felt in public. She couldn't help wondering what it would be like to live near Hasting's Corner. To shop here every week. To go to the high school basketball games and the Fourth of July parades.

To live in a real home, not an apartment, with a nice kitchen and a big bed....

The image of Luke came to her as vividly as the produce sign. He was wearing jeans, that's all, and he was smiling at her with genuine pleasure.

Her throat tightened with a want so real it hurt. She hurried to the check out to get away from her stupid fantasies. Her? In a town this small? Everyone sticking their nose into her business?

Not a chance.

Look at the trouble Luke was going to because he didn't want people knowing he was back. It wasn't the anonymous city. It was the land of busybodies and snoops, and she, for one, wouldn't last a week here.

After paying for her groceries, she put the bags in the back seat and headed out of the sea of trucks. When she got to Main Street, she turned right instead of left. She wasn't even sure why, except that she was crazy from the heat.

Nearby was the variety store, probably still owned by the old woman with arthritic fingers. As a child,

Annie had been fascinated by her, by how she adapted to her fate. Despite her misshapen hands, she'd stocked supplies, counted out pennies and done it all with kindness.

The post office had the old statue of George Hastings, who'd been some kind of civil war hero, right in front. The trees in the park seemed greener, bigger, but the community bulletin board was as messy as she remembered.

There were kids on bikes, on skateboards, and the only difference Annie could see from her previous visits was that they had cell phones plastered to their ears or ear buds blasting music from their iPods.

And there were baby carriages. Lots of those. While she might be feeling nostalgic and weepy she wasn't nuts. No way would she join the Mommy Brigade. Not her.

She was a cop. A city cop. And no good-looking cowboy, no matter how mysterious, was enough to make her change her ways.

She turned at the next corner and headed to the ranch. If the guys didn't like lasagna, they could damn well fix their own dinner.

LUKE DUCKED BEHIND the china cupboard when he heard the car coming toward the house, but it was Annie, back from her trip to town. It had been difficult to let her go without a reminder to keep his presence here a secret, but he'd had to. She was already suspicious.

He'd gotten a lot done in her absence and while it was nice that he'd be able to show off his work, he'd done his shoulder no favors.

He headed to the car, purposely walking on the new steps he'd finished. Annie got out of her car and instantly he knew something was wrong. Guilt stabbed him in the gut and it was just like old times. He didn't even have to ask, he knew he'd done something wrong. Everybody knew he wasn't worth the boots on his feet. It was always his fault, at least out here.

It didn't matter that years had gone by, that this town was no longer his home. Seeing Annie's tight expression and her jerky movements as she got the bags out of the backseat, he knew someone in town had gotten to her.

He thought about leaving. Just getting in his truck and riding into the sunset. The hell with clearing his name. What good would it do, anyway? He might avoid being accused of stealing a million, but his older crimes, real and imagined, would never be expunged. Not in Hasting's Corner.

"You gonna stand there all afternoon, or you gonna let me in the house?"

Luke jumped when he realized she was only a foot away. "Sorry," he said, moving aside.

She didn't speak as she passed him. It was only when she reached the door that it dawned on him he hadn't taken the bags from her. Hurrying up the stairs he reached to help, but Annie jerked away. "What are you doing?"

"Helping."

"I've got it."

"But—"

"I've been carrying my own groceries for a long time, Luke," she said. Then she entered the kitchen, her back straight, her head held high.

He followed, not liking how much she sounded like a police officer. "Did something happen?"

"What do you mean?" she asked.

"In town. You seem upset."

"I'm not." She took a big red box of frozen lasagna out of the bag and put it on the counter.

"Really," he said, letting her know he was on to her.

"I'm not upset. Dinner should be ready in—" she turned the box over "—about an hour."

Luke moved close to her as she pulled the rest of the food from the brown bags. For a cop, she didn't mask her feelings well. Her cheeks were flushed, her lips tight and there was a fire in her eyes that should have been lit by kisses, not some gossip relayed in the frozen foods section. Something had to be done, and right quick.

As Anne reached to turn the oven on, her shirt hiked up to show a thin strip of pale flesh above the waist of her jeans.

He moved in to press his front against her back, spanning her bare skin with his hands. "Can I be of assistance?"

He felt her shiver. Her hand froze midair and he took that as a yes. Honestly, he had no interest in helping her with supper. Not when he could breathe in the soft apple scent of her hair or taste the delicate flesh beneath her ear.

"What are you doing?" she asked. She didn't sound like a cop now.

"I was thinking about you," he said, and he took her pink lobe between his teeth.

Her shoulder rose, but she didn't make him stop. "Thinking what?"

"How sweet you taste." He paused. "Like spun honey."

She pushed back slightly, moving that nice round bottom of hers against his rapidly swelling hard-on. "I don't."

"Now, darlin', in this instance, I think I'm a better judge than you."

She sighed. "Fine. I taste like a damn sugar cookie."

He nibbled on her neck and wondered if she could feel his smile. But when he turned her around and took her mouth, there wasn't a thing to smile about. Hunger only, and not for dinner, not for anything, but for this woman. This stranger from the east who was becoming more troublesome with each moment, each touch.

His hands went to her blouse as he thrust into the heat of her mouth. He undid one button, then another and another, until the shirt was no longer an obstacle. Her bra was next, but that was easy for a man who, from the age of thirteen, had studied its removal.

He slipped his hands under the loosened cups.

Her warm breasts made his knees weak and he leaned against her, wanting more, but teasing himself with his palms against the hard peaks of her nipples.

Something banged behind him, but he didn't give a damn. That is, before he felt Annie stiffen in his arms. Before he saw her eyes widen, horrified.

Before he heard Chester's embarrassed cough, followed by the screen door slamming shut.

8

ANNIE PULLED AWAY, shaking her head. She went to the window and watched Chester hobble toward his dusty white pickup truck. "I thought he was gone."

"Yeah, I did, too." Luke came up behind her and pulled her back against his chest. He was still hard. "But he's gone now."

"That's not the point." She briefly closed her eyes, letting the heat of his body wash over her like a warm bath. But she wouldn't get too comfortable. Not until Chester's truck was out of sight. Not until she couldn't even see the dust his tires were kicking up. "The poor guy must think we're a couple of dogs in heat."

"So?"

"So?" She spun around to face him, only they were too close and the friction caused by the sudden move made her breasts tingle. Made her forget that Chester's truck wasn't out of sight yet. "You won't say *so* when he turns a hose on us."

Luke didn't even smile. He took her face in his hands and kissed her. She laid her hands on his chest, kissing him back, until the rhythm changed and he pushed his tongue between her parted lips. There was no mistaking what he wanted. But did she want it, too?

His thumbs brushed her cheeks as he explored her mouth. He was an amazingly good kisser. He didn't try to swallow her whole, or slobber or try to suck her tongue like an overactive vacuum. No, Luke had been around this block many a time, and he'd learned his lessons well.

Some small part of her felt as if she should be bothered by his expertise, but the rest of her, the important parts, weren't complaining.

She could relax for the first time in years, knowing she was in excellent hands. Astonishing hands, as she was just beginning to see.

He'd stopped cradling her head and moved one arm around her back, pulling her close enough to feel the erection beneath his jeans.

Her cynical mind waited for him to show off. But he didn't do any weird pushing or humping. He was too busy kissing and nipping the side of her neck. It was an odd sensation, the way he sort of nibbled on her. It gave her goosebumps. That particular part of her neck, right below her ear, must have some interesting wiring, because she could feel the sensations right down to her toes.

Was this something only cowboys knew about? Or had she simply been with men who hadn't taken the time to learn what works on a woman's body. Yeah, they all knew the major stuff. Hell, she'd been encouraged when the clitoris had come out of the closet, so to speak, and gotten the attention of the men in her neck of the woods.

The fact was, she'd never realized the sweet spot on her neck could make her whole body take notice.

Luke chuckled. Even that was a new experience. He left his lips on her, and she felt his soft vibration.

"What's so funny?" she asked.

"Darlin', I love the sounds you make."

"Sounds?"

He chuckled again. "Never mind. You're just a real treat, that's all." He licked a long line between her shoulder and the base of her ear. "Tasty, too."

Annie hadn't even realized she'd been making noise. It surprised her because she'd had complaints. Not that she was loud, but that she didn't make any noise at all.

This was turning into the most unexpected trip. And if Luke could do all this magic standing up, what would it be like when they were in bed?

That very second, Luke pulled back. "What do you say we take this to another room?"

She wondered if he minded that he was the one doing all the dazzling. "I'd like that."

His smile told her he didn't mind in the least.

LUKE WOULD HAVE PREFERRED taking her to neutral territory—not to her aunt's bedroom—but he could work with it. With such a responsive partner, he could have made it work on a bus bench, so he supposed Aunt Marjorie's gingham wasn't so bad.

Annie had surprised him. He'd figured she would have been suspicious as hell and that she'd never go to the bedroom this quickly. Although, he supposed it was his own prejudice that had painted that picture. Her being a cop and all.

But now that he thought about it, from their first touch, she'd been willing. A little shy, but that was understandable.

"Let me do that," he offered, moving around in back of her as she stood by the bed. He took the bottom of her shirt and pulled it over her head, leaving her in shorts and her neat white bra.

That was something different. The women he knew bought their duds at Victoria's Secret and other places like that, and they always went way overboard. He didn't have the heart to tell them he couldn't care less if they had matching bras and panties. His goal was to have them naked as quickly as humanly possible. The same goal applied even if they'd been wearing potato sacks.

He liked the women underneath though and, when he undid Annie's bra, then slipped those bands off her shoulders, he was treated to something mighty special.

Her body appealed to him in a special way. Annie's long, lean frame was strong, with the kind of muscles that defined her as a woman instead of making her look masculine.

Now, those breasts…

He moved in front of her and cupped her with his

palms. She was small and his hand was big, and that might not appeal to all men. But as he stood there, bringing no pressure to bear, he felt her nipples grow hard and ripe. It was like magic. Like watching flowers blossom.

She got his attention when she pulled his shirt out of his jeans.

"Don't look so shocked," she said. "I'm not doing this dance alone."

"No, ma'am, you are not," he said. In two shakes, he'd toed off his boots and his socks, had his shirt off, his belt undone and he was reaching for his zipper.

Annie laughed, but she got with the program. He watched her strip off her shorts—no, her panties didn't match—and then she was naked and if he'd been hard two seconds ago, he was now in danger of losing all the blood from his brain.

He pulled her to him with both arms, then let them both fall onto the bed. Old springs squeaked beneath them, but he didn't care, not when his skin was on fire from the feel of her against him.

"Luke?"

"Yeah?"

"Tell me you brought protection."

"What?"

She looked up at him with wide eyes. "Protection?"

"Oh, yeah. Don't you worry."

She smiled all pretty and sweet at him. "I'll stop worrying when you show me the condom."

He had to give it to her. She knew what she wanted and wasn't afraid to say what's what.

"Yes, ma'am."

"And Luke?"

"Yeah?"

"If you don't stop calling me ma'am, I'm going to have to hurt you."

He laughed. "I believe it. Now, you wait right there while I get that condom you're so interested in. Maybe you'd feel even better if you were to help me put it on."

She moved her hand down his body, grasping the base of his cock in her palm. "Since I have something decent to work with, yes, I think I might."

He kissed her, waited until she let go, then he got his jeans from the floor. He always kept a couple of condoms in his wallet, which hadn't always been a blessing, but today, he was damn happy for his good habits.

He turned back to Annie, who rested her head on her hand, watching, and presented her the packet with a bit of fanfare.

She plucked it from his hand, ripped the thing open with her teeth, and said, "Come on over, *darlin'*, if you dare."

Her Southern accent wasn't so hot, but the rest of her sizzled. He laid down so fast interesting things bounced, but it didn't matter. All he wanted was more—more touching, more kissing—and a lot more condoms.

ANNIE COULDN'T BELIEVE how she ached. It was almost painful to want him this much, but just as painful to make him stop this.

He had her on her back, and her nipple was between his teeth, his tongue as fast as a hummingbird's wings, flicking her bud. That would have made her crazy enough, but his fingers were inside her and he was teasing her clit in a way that made her want to scream.

Pressure, release, fast, slow, all of it designed to drive a woman right out of her mind.

With all the strength she had left, she clamped her hand onto his wrist. "Luke. Stop."

His head rose immediately. "Am I hurting you?"

"No. Yes. Listen, are you gonna do it or not?"

His expression changed from worried to cocky, and she would have punched him if she didn't want him so badly.

"Oh, Annie. You do have a way with words."

"Make fun of me later," she said. She spread her legs in what, for her, was an amazingly blatant gesture.

He looked down, then back at her face. Something must have gotten through, because he got up on his knees and climbed between her legs. He met her gaze and never let it go as he brought the head of his cock to her swollen lips. A quick rub and then he entered her, barely. "You ready?"

"Dammit, Luke—" She gasped as he thrust into her—hard. She'd been on the edge of coming for the last twenty minutes. She wasn't on the edge anymore.

"Nice," he whispered as he pulled back, then thrust again.

She was squeezing him, all her muscles tightening as she came. Her back arched, her toes pointed and she cried out so loud they probably heard her in town.

She'd never had any man do this to her. This wasn't just sex. It was something not in the dictionary. Not in the history of words. And certainly not in her language.

Maybe it was all cowboys, but she doubted it. No, this was pure Luke McCall, and for tonight, he was all hers.

IF ANNIE HAD HER WAY, she'd tear down the faded curtains and order new ones from a catalog. But this wasn't her kitchen and she had to respect her aunt's things. Which meant the best Annie could do was mend some of the frayed edges. Not that she was any good with a needle. In fact, she'd probably sewn only three things in her life. But she'd give it a try.

She set the sewing basket she'd found at the foot of her aunt's bed on the kitchen table. The strain of lifting her arms surprised her, because the basket wasn't heavy.

Her skin was so sensitive—as if she'd scrubbed with a loofah too long. It tingled with a memory all its own, forcing her to relive snatches of last night. Certainly not an unpleasant experience, but hardly practical while she was standing on a step stool, taking down curtains to be mended.

Last night had been an experience she wasn't likely to forget. Not even if the hottest hunk showed up at the doorstep of her drab Brooklyn brownstone apartment, stripped naked. For someone like Annie, last night was a once in a lifetime deal.

"Annie, I'm gonna go get—"

She turned too quickly at the sound of Luke's voice and nearly fell backward off the stepstool. Instantly, he was there, anchoring her with his hands around her waist, keeping her steady. Even though she could have easily gotten down by herself, he lifted her in the air and then set her on the floor. He jerked his shoulder and tried to hide the grimace of pain.

"Luke." She lightly touched his arm.

"It's okay." He stretched his shoulder and winced again. Then he gave her a lopsided smile. "I'm actually fishing for another rubdown."

Her heart rate accelerated. "You got it."

He moved closer for a kiss. "Tonight?"

Now, if he wanted. But they had work to do with only a short time to accomplish a lot. "Tonight," she agreed.

His gaze lowered to her mouth, to her breasts. Then he blinked and met her eyes. "I'd better go. We need more fencing and a wheelbarrow that doesn't fall over every time you park it." Luke shook his head and Annie smiled. "If you give me a list, I'll get whatever else we need."

"Want me to go with you?"

"Nah." He looked away, pretending to check out

the curtains. "I'm going over to Melbourne. They have a big hardware store there. But it's in the next county, over an hour away, so it may take a while."

Something was wrong. It wasn't just that he was a lousy liar, but instinct told her he was hiding something. Maybe it was because he didn't want to go to town, but she didn't think that was all there was to it. He'd already admitted he wanted to keep a low profile. "I guess the smart thing for me to do is stay here and work on the curtains."

He nodded. "Good. I'll pick up some take-out on the way back."

She watched him walk out the door, a bit apprehensive that he might not come back. And if he didn't, so what? She had no emotional investment in him. Although, the sex had been great and more would be nice and of course his help around the ranch had already made a difference.

She went up the stepstool to finish unhooking the curtains, heard the door open and turned to see Luke heading straight for her.

"I forgot something." He pulled her down and hauled her against him. Her head automatically went back so she could look at him. He kissed her—hard, deep, satisfying—then pulled away to brush her cheek with his fingertips. "I'll be back as soon as I can."

She lifted herself on tiptoes and kissed him again. "Hurry."

One side of his mouth curved up. "Yes, ma'am."

In those few seconds he'd gotten hard and she

needed only to move her hips the slightest bit to
urge him on. But she didn't want Chester catching
them again and they really did have a lot of work
to do. Tonight. She could wait. "Get out of here,"
she whispered.

He pushed the hair from the side of her neck and
touched her skin with his lips. "You sure?"

"No. Now go."

He smiled, and this time he did leave.

LUKE DROVE AS FAST as the old pickup would go.
Damn, his Corvette would have gotten him to Ne-
braska by now, if not to the county line. But, out of
desperation, he'd traded his baby for Tyler Scoggins'
beat up, but totally anonymous pickup truck. For two
weeks only. That was the deal. All he could hope for
was that the stupid kid didn't wrap himself around a
pole with it.

Out of habit he glanced at the dashboard looking
for the time, but the truck didn't even have a clock.
Hell, the air-conditioning barely worked and, of
course, this had to be the hottest May he could remember. Or maybe it *seemed* hot because he'd been
working outside for a change, not sitting in some bar
drinking beer and flirting with the cocktail wait-
resses, trying to figure out which one he'd take home
with him for the night.

Women had never been in short supply for him.
Especially not after he'd started winning buckles and
large purses. He wasn't dumb enough to think it was

all about him…. Maybe, when he was younger, he'd been fooled. Mostly because he'd been too full of himself to see things plainly.

But after his first sixteen years of listening to how much he looked like his father and how he would probably end up a no-account deadbeat just like him, the attention had been nice. After a few years on his own, the sound of his mother's screeching voice had started to fade. Granddad's silence was what still echoed in his head.

Even though he had to know it was wrong to yell at a kid all the time, the old man never said a word, never once defended Luke, his only grandson. The thing was, they got along, him and Granddad. They'd fished together, done chores together and he'd taught Luke how to ride a horse. Even put the idea of riding rodeo in Luke's head. But, when it came down to taking his side, Granddad always walked away.

A rabbit darted across the two-lane highway, and Luke swerved to avoid hitting it. Good thing there'd been no oncoming traffic.

He took a deep breath and forced his concentration on the road. Thinking like that wasn't gonna do him any good. Past history. Nothing to do with now. He needed to keep his head clear. Needed to worry about how he was gonna get to Joanne short of stalking the Seabrook estate 24/7.

Maybe today he'd get lucky. It was Sunday and Joanne usually pretended to go to church. Conveniently, Miguel, aka King Kong, the Seabrooks' driver, had Sundays off. So Joanne had always driven herself so that no one knew she was actually meeting Luke. Maybe the woman was crazy enough to show up at their usual place and time. She wasn't stupid, but she was a thrill seeker, and Luke couldn't afford to ignore any opportunity to get to her.

He got near the motel but, instead of pulling into the parking lot, he coasted by, squinting into the sun, trying to find the black Lincoln sedan with the gold hood ornament in the crowded lot. He even drove around the corner and checked out the part of the lot closer to the coffee shop where semitrucks often parked for the night. No good. But that didn't mean she couldn't still show up. He glanced at his watch. Five minutes early.

Next to the gas station across the street was a vacant wooded lot, and he parked at the edge of the trees to wait. After ten minutes of smelling frying bacon from the diner, his patience slipped. His stomach rumbled and, after so little sleep last night, he badly needed coffee. He yawned, adjusted his hat to block the sun creeping west then yawned again. A triple shot of caffeine straight into the bloodstream would be even better.

Best of all would be a big piece of Annie a la mode.

But why did he have to think about last night? About Annie? Wasn't he in enough trouble—because of a woman? Except, Annie wasn't like most of the women he knew. She was smart and independent and she didn't care how many championship buckles he'd won. He doubted she'd even recognize the significance of a buckle.

What a body, too. Lean and firm, but still enough curves to keep things interesting. What he remembered most, though, were the soft sounds she'd made. Kind of breathy sighs that turned into sexy groans. Damn if he wasn't getting hard. He shifted positions and touched his fly.

"Señor Luke?"

At the sound of the heavily accented feminine voice, he jumped and jerked his hand away. One of the Seabrooks' maids stood not a foot away. Fortunately, not the evil sister. Although he almost didn't recognize the woman without the ridiculous black and white ruffled uniform Seabrook made her wear.

Margarita moved back, her big dark eyes widening. "I am very sorry, señor. I did not mean to scare you."

"You didn't. I was just—" He shook his head. "What are you doing here?"

"Mrs. Seabrook. She sent me."

No way. He got out of the truck, and she moved farther back to accommodate him. "What for?"

The young woman blushed, her cheeks matching her modest rose-colored dress. "I have a message."

He felt bad. His tone had been unnecessarily harsh. It wasn't her fault Joanne hadn't shown up herself. "Want to go across the street to the coffee shop? I'll buy you breakfast while you give me the message."

She blinked, her pink-tinted lips lifting in a shy smile. "I am on my way to church."

"Ah."

She shrugged her thin shoulders. "There is not much to say. Only that she cannot help you." She smoothed back her shiny black hair and tucked the strays into the bun at her nape. With obvious reluctance, she added, "And that it would be better if you left the country."

Luke stared at the woman and had to remind himself not to shoot the messenger. Leave the country? Was Joanne out of her mind? How was he supposed to do that, even if he wanted to? Which he didn't. It would take a lot of money to— Did she actually think that he had stolen the million bucks?

"Señor Luke?" Margarita gingerly touched his hand to get his attention. "Mr. Seabrook, he is very angry. He screams your name every night when he is talking on the phone and calls you very bad names. Maybe Señora Seabrook is right."

Luke choked back a curse. Margarita was only trying to help. "Do you know why he's mad?"

She slowly nodded.

"Do you think I stole the money?"

Her eyes widened in horror, and she briskly shook her head.

He squeezed her hand and she blushed again. "Thank you for believing me."

She kept her gaze on the ground, but she was smiling. "You want me to give Mrs. Seabrook a message?" she asked, her smile gone as soon as she mentioned Joanne's name.

Luke laughed without humor. Lifting his hat, he raked a hand through his hair. Hell, what was there to say? She clearly would rather see him hang than admit to their affair. He thought for a moment and then smiled. "Tell her I said nothing."

She frowned. "Señor?"

"Tell her I listened and then I walked away." Let her stew. Wonder about what his next move would be. "Would you do that for me, Margarita?"

She moistened her lips and smoothed her hair in that same nervous gesture. Then she nodded, briefly closed her eyes and made the sign of the cross. "Mrs. Seabrook," she whispered, "she is not a nice lady." Then she hurried toward the street.

He watched her enter the crosswalk, thinking about what she'd said. Shy, quiet Margarita wasn't one to talk about her employer, or about anyone else for that matter, and he could tell the words hadn't come easily for her. Good reason to pay attention.

Maybe he was going about this the wrong way. Maybe it was Seabrook himself who Luke should be going after. But first he'd better get a gun.

9

ANNIE HAD JUST FINISHED the bedroom curtains when she heard Luke's truck coming down the gravel drive, much earlier than she'd expected. The heat had really gotten to her and she'd wanted to grab a shower before he got back. Instead, she hurried into the bathroom, splashed her face, used her finger to rub toothpaste across her teeth and then brushed her hair.

She got to the kitchen just as the truck parked. Only it wasn't his truck. This one was much bigger and newer and hunter green. The tinted windows prevented her from seeing the driver, and then the door opened and a woman got out. Around thirty, long blond hair and wearing too much makeup, she came around the front of the truck in jeans that were ridiculously tight and low riding, exposing an inch of skin around her belly.

The woman looked around as she approached the porch, craning her neck to see what or who was in the barn. Annie opened the front door and stepped outside. The woman didn't see her at first but when she did, she frowned.

"Hi." Annie carefully avoided a sagging board, and let the screen door close behind her.

"Mornin'." The woman smiled and then tilted her head to look past Annie into the house. "Is Luke around?" she asked in a southern drawl much more pronounced than Luke's.

"Who?"

Abruptly, the woman looked back at her, a condescending smile curving her bright pink lips. "It's okay. I know he's here, but I haven't told anyone else."

Annie didn't know what to say. Not that she wanted to lie for Luke.

"I'm Sally Jo McIntosh, Billy's mother. Who are you?"

No sense denying Luke was staying here. "Annie," she said abruptly, ignoring the curiosity on the other woman's face. "Luke isn't here right now. Would you like me to give him a message?"

Clearly annoyed, Sally Jo checked her watch. "Do you know when he'll be back?"

"No clue."

Sally Jo sighed loudly. "Tell him to call me, will ya? But it has to be before seven-thirty. It's real important." She glanced around again, as if she didn't believe he really wasn't there. Then she looked again at Annie and smiled. "Thank you, and you have a real nice day."

Annie watched her make her way back to the truck, listening to her cuss softly as her high heels crunched deep into the gravel. Sally Jo started the big truck and gunned the engine a couple of times before reversing into the turnaround in front of the huge red oak and then she headed down the driveway toward the main road.

Hoping the noise hadn't woken Chester, who hadn't come home until after dawn, Annie went back inside, poured a glass of lemonade and took it to the living room. Not even noon and it was already so hot that she had the air conditioner and every fan in the house going full blast. She dreaded the thought of working outside later, but that she would be with Luke made it a whole lot better.

Instead of concentrating on what needed to be done, her thoughts went back to Sally Jo. Was she an old girlfriend of Luke's looking to start up again? She was Billy's mother, but that didn't mean she was married. And damn it, this *was* Annie's business, because the sex had been awesome last night and she didn't want to share.

She took a sip of the icy lemonade and then lifted her face to the whirling fan sitting on the end table. The air wasn't nearly cool enough, but it still felt good hitting her sticky skin. The sky hadn't lightened up all morning and part of her wished it would rain. Release some of the humidity. Give them an excuse not to work outside. They could stay in and cuddle, have mind-blowing sex again.

This idea alone sent *her* thermostat soaring, but the thought of how much work still had to be done cooled her off quickly. Fixing the porch was important. It was a hazard.

As soon as Luke came back with the lumber, they'd tackle those two things. He didn't seem to think it would take more than a day.

Annie straightened when she thought she heard something. The fan was too loud so she switched it off. An engine purred. She got up and headed for the kitchen. It couldn't be Luke. His truck wasn't that smooth.

A black sports car was parked near the steps. The door opened and a woman climbed out. Tall, blonde and stunning. Annie gritted her teeth. Another one of Luke's fans, no doubt.

LUKE DIDN'T GET BACK until three-fifteen, a lot later than he'd planned. He left the lumber in the truck and went inside to look for Annie. The aroma of freshly baked apple pie filled the kitchen. The source sat on the stove beside two foil-covered casserole dishes. He got closer and smelled lasagna, too. His stomach rumbled.

Annie walked in, her hair piled messily on top of her head, several loose strands curling around her flushed face. Her shorts were rolled up almost to the point of indecency, making his pulse speed. "I didn't hear you."

"Just got here." He met her halfway and caught her around the waist. Pulling her against him, he kissed her but, although she seemed willing enough, something was wrong. He coaxed her lips open but the enthusiasm wasn't quite there. "Hey," he said, drawing back, looking at her. "It took longer than I expected. I probably should've called."

She smiled. "It's okay. I figured you'd be a while. How much was the lumber?"

"I forget. The receipt's in the truck." He gestured to the stove. "You've been busy."

"Not me." She shrugged her shoulders and went to the table and picked up a pad of paper. "Let's see…the apple pie and chicken and dumplings are from Barb. The lasagna is from Janice. Sally Jo and Melinda didn't bring you anything, but they want you to call. In fact, they all asked that you call." She handed him the list, her face expressionless. "Sally Jo is the only one who didn't leave her number. I figured you have it."

Luke stared at the scribbling. Did the whole goddamn town know he was here? When he got a hold of that Billy, he was gonna kick his scrawny…

"I had no idea you were so popular." Annie went to the fridge and got out the pitcher of lemonade. "You're quite the celebrity."

"Yeah, right."

"Did you even know you have a fan club?" Her back was to him as she got out two glasses, her posture as rigid as a branding iron.

Obviously, there was no telling what one of those women had said about him. He tore off the top sheet, crumpled it in his fist and tossed it into the trash can under the sink. So much for laying low. Now what was he gonna do?

Get FREE BOOKS and FREE GIFTS when you play the...

LAS VEGAS

GAME

Just scratch off the gold box with a coin. Then check below to see the gifts you get!

YES! I have scratched off the gold box. Please send me my **2 FREE BOOKS** and **2 FREE GIFTS** for which I qualify. I understand that I am under no obligation to purchase any books as explained on the back of this card.

◄ DETACH AND MAIL CARD TODAY! ►

© 2001 HARLEQUIN ENTERPRISES LTD.
® and ™ are trademarks owned and used by the licensee.

351 HDL EL42   151 HDL ELVF

FIRST NAME   LAST NAME

ADDRESS

APT.#   CITY

STATE/PROV.   ZIP/POSTAL CODE   (H-B-03/07)

7	7	7	Worth TWO FREE BOOKS plus TWO BONUS Mystery Gifts!
🍒	🍒	🍒	Worth TWO FREE BOOKS!
🔔	🔔	♣	TRY AGAIN!

www.eHarlequin.com

Offer limited to one per household and not valid to current Harlequin® Blaze® subscribers. All orders subject to approval.

Your Privacy - Harlequin Books is committed to protecting your privacy. Our privacy policy is available online at www.eHarlequin.com or upon request from the Harlequin Reader Service. From time to time we make our lists of customers available to reputable firms who may have a product or service of interest to you. If you would prefer for us not to share your name and address, please check here. ☐

The Harlequin Reader Service® — Here's how it works:

She glanced at him, and then her gaze went to the trash can. "I wouldn't do that if I were you."

"I'm not calling them."

"Then they'll just show up again. But if you call and tell them you're passing through and that you're leaving tonight, they might back off."

"What did you tell them?"

"Only that you weren't here."

She had a point. He retrieved the paper.

"For what it's worth, each one said they hadn't told anyone else you're here."

The humor in her voice should have been reassuring, only it irritated the hell out of him. But that wasn't fair, because she didn't know the stakes. She didn't understand that this meant he had to leave.

ANNIE HOVERED near the bedroom door, knowing she probably shouldn't have been listening. Oh, hell, no probably about it. He'd used the bedroom phone because he wanted privacy, even though it had been her idea to call everyone.

Why she even persisted was beyond her. This was his third call. Same sweet-talking spiel. The delivery was so smooth it gave her a shiver. The guy was a born con artist. And worse, he attracted women like bees to honey. So what did he see in Annie? Convenience? A safe harbor that he could leave as soon as it no longer suited his purpose?

She was about to return to the kitchen when she heard him laugh, and the deep husky sound stopped her. The other two calls had been brief. He'd assured the women how sorry he was that he couldn't see them this time and promised he'd call on his way back through town.

His tone was different this time and he didn't seem in a hurry to get off the phone. Disgusted with herself, but unable to resist, Annie stepped closer to the bedroom door.

"Come on now, darlin', don't take it personally. I didn't even know I was coming to town until the last minute." Luke paused. "Nobody. Honest. She's the widow's niece, that's all." Another silence. "No, that's not true. I stopped to help Chester with something."

Annie took a deep, stinging breath. What was she doing? This wasn't like her. Why was she putting up with this? She ought to kick him out right now. Obviously, he wouldn't have trouble finding another bed. Part of her understood that he needed to placate these women, but she hated the lying and manipulation. Like her father. Like Steve Witherspoon.

"Yeah, of course Annie is pretty," he said. "But I didn't know she was gonna be here." And then in a tone not so congenial, he added, "Besides, I'm not married, Sally Jo. You are."

Damn, one minute she was ready to throw him out and the next she wanted to drag him back to bed. She started to walk away and heard him hang up. Quickly, she went down the hall to the kitchen and grabbed a dish towel and wiped a dry glass furiously, waiting for him.

Hearing him approach, she looked over her shoulder. "Any ideas for dinner?"

He pushed a frustrated hand through his hair. "Man, I'm gonna kill Billy."

She put the glass in the cupboard. "You don't think those calls did the trick?"

"The thing is, Billy's coming back and he'll see that I'm still here and shoot his mouth off again."

"Chester told Billy he didn't have to come back until next week." She stopped, wanted to say more but didn't want to reveal that she'd been listening to his phone conversations. "Anyway, if I were one of those women I'd get the hint and back off."

Luke smiled and slowly moved toward her. "But you're nothing like them." He lifted her chin and kissed her gently. "That's what I like about you."

"Not to mention I'm a safe harbor and a good cover," she said, not bothering to hide her irritation.

"Now, why would you say a thing like that?" He pulled her against him and then backed her up until her butt hit the counter. Her heart raced when he braced his hands on either side of her, effectively trapping her. Not that she planned on going anywhere.

A slow smile warmed his blue eyes and made lines fan out at the corners. "So?"

Good question. One she really didn't want to think about. Not now, anyway. Not with the heat of his erection nearly singeing her belly and making her so wet it could turn embarrassing.

He kept his hands where they were, lowered his

head and kissed the side of her neck. Annie closed her eyes. What harm was there in enjoying a few days of terrific recreational sex? They both knew there was a time limit. No promises or expectations were required. When would she get an opportunity like this again? Never.

"Hey."

She opened her eyes. Luke was looking at her, his eyes so dark they hardly looked blue.

"I have an idea," he said, and then groaned when she moved against him.

She smiled with satisfaction. "What's that?"

"Let's go somewhere."

"Now?"

He moved his hand persuasively to her breast.

"What about work?"

"Later. When it's cooler."

"But…" Through her blouse he touched her nipple, circling his thumb over the hard nub. She bit her lower lip, trying to remember what they'd been talking about.

"Think about it… No one around for miles," he whispered, and then kissed her right below her earlobe.

"How do you know?"

"It's my secret place."

Right. Where he'd taken Sally Jo and Barb and every other female in Hasting's Corner. So, what did she care? For her, this was about sex. Great sex that she wouldn't be getting much more of, so now wasn't the time to get stupid.

He unfastened the top button of her blouse and trailed his tongue across her collarbone. "Annie," he murmured, "you're all I want."

How THE HELL was he gonna tell her? He had to leave by tomorrow morning. Luke watched Annie's eyes widen when the lake came into view. Her lips parted and then curved. The pink in her cheeks was probably from working outside yesterday. She leaned forward, moving her head so she could get a panoramic view of the water lapping the shore and the surrounding forest.

The scene looked like a movie set that someone had spent weeks trying to perfect: each tree was the ideal size and shape, the sky was a crystal-clear blue and even the small boulders that cropped up along the water's edge looked as if they'd been fussed over.

Funny, he'd been here over a hundred times and never looked at it like that before. He'd been young when he'd come here after school, trying to get laid or escaping his mother's crazy ranting. She was good at it. Hell, no wonder his father had run off.

But that was in the past, and Luke wouldn't let bad memories ruin today. Annie's awestruck expression had made him take a second look, let him see the land differently. He parked the truck on the rocky ground, as close to the lake as he could get without disturbing things, and stared out over the water.

They both sat quietly for a few minutes, and then Annie asked, "How did you ever find this place?"

He shrugged. "By accident, while I was riding my bike after school."

"But isn't this far?"

"Not as the crow flies." He opened his door. "Let's find a spot before it gets crowded."

She frowned at him.

He touched the tip of her nose. "I'm kidding."

"Maybe not. You haven't been here in a long time."

"True, but this is still out of the way enough that most people wouldn't know about it. Besides…" He winked. "We're trespassing."

"Oh, great."

At the exasperated look on her face he laughed. "Don't worry about it. The owner lives in Dallas. Come on."

He got out of the truck and then grabbed the basket they'd packed. Annie followed him, carrying their towels, even though she'd insisted she wouldn't go swimming because she didn't have a swimsuit. He'd see about that.

"This okay?" he asked, stopping at a small clearing that looked relatively rock-free, and kicked away the few pebbles that would make sitting uncomfortable.

She nodded, then her gaze caught on something across the lake. "There's something in there," she said, taking a step back.

"In the water?"

She nodded again.

He grinned. "That's just Big Foot taking a swim."

"Very funny."

"They're called fish, darlin'. They actually live in lakes out here in the country."

She gave him a flat look and shook out her towel.

"Uh-uh, don't lay that on the ground. You'll need it to dry off. I brought a blanket to sit on."

"I told you I don't have a suit."

"Don't need one."

"Right." Shaking her head, she stepped back so he could spread the blanket.

"I'm serious. You don't see me packing one."

Her gaze dropped to his fly, and then quickly raised. Their eyes met, then she abruptly turned away. "Bet you brought many sweet young things here back in the day."

"A couple."

"Right." She folded her towel in thirds and placed it on the blanket, then sat on it.

He dropped down beside her. "Actually, I liked coming here alone. I loved the quiet."

"You have a lot of brothers and sisters?"

He stared at her, looking for any quirk of the mouth or knowing gleam in her eyes. But hell, she didn't know anything about him. Chester would be the only one who could fill her in and he wouldn't do that. "No," he said finally. "Just me."

She stared back for a moment, plainly curious, but she didn't say a word.

"My mother." The words were out of his mouth before he knew what he was saying. He drew in a sharp breath, annoyed that he'd mentioned this sore subject.

"Ah," she said with a single slow nod.

He waited for her to start with the questions. All she did was draw her legs up until her chin rested on her knees and she gazed out at the water. The hint of a bittersweet smile rested on her lips.

Christ, she got it. She understood his turmoil, his shame, the frustration he'd felt as a child. His heart started to pound. He knew deep in his gut that she got it. He didn't know how but… "You have one of those, too?"

She nodded, her mouth twisting wryly. "My father."

He picked up a pebble and skipped it across the water. It sunk after the second skip. He'd lost his touch. Or, maybe it was because his hands weren't so steady.

"Is she still alive?" Annie asked softly.

"Last I heard."

"Your father?"

"Oh, yeah." She snorted. "Of course, I only hear from him when he needs something. What about your dad?"

He picked up another pebble. This was new territory for him. Luke never talked about his father. Refused to even think about him. "Never met the man."

She didn't seem shocked, nor did she get that pitiful look on her face that he'd expected. She sighed. "I never met my mom. No, I did, but I was three when she left, so I don't remember her at all."

"Seriously?"

She looked at him. "Would I lie about something like that?"

"No, I mean, it's kind of weird that we both have a parent who left."

"Yeah." She turned her face back at the water. "It's not something I generally talk about."

"Me, neither. To tell you the truth, I'm not sure why I spilled the beans."

"Okay." Her mouth curved slightly. "Now we have something else in common."

He laughed, still feeling uneasy. "Where's your mother now?"

"Dead."

"Sorry."

"Don't be. I didn't know her. Thanks to my father." Annie fidgeted, as if she regretted adding that piece of information. He totally understood.

"He run her off?"

She shook her head. "She headed for Hollywood. Wanted to be a star, instead of a wife and mother. She didn't make it, though. She was killed in a car crash on the way there." She looked at Luke then, her eyes glassy. "The bastard didn't even tell me. I found out on my own, when I was nineteen."

Luke exhaled slowly. "So you had been thinking the whole time that she was maybe coming back."

Her lips pressed tightly together, Annie nodded.

He didn't try to get her to talk. It was easy enough to read between the lines. He understood the longing of a child. The soul-deep craving for love and attention and the hope to someday be rescued.

As a kid, he used to imagine his father riding

on a huge black stallion across the pasture where Granddad's cattle had to be rounded up. Luke always took an extra long time out there, hoping his mother would either have gone out or gone to bed. But usually she was there, waiting, yelling, telling him how worthless he was. Reminding him that he was like his lowlife father and screaming so loud everyone in the county had to have heard her.

Not once had she said a decent thing about his father. Made a boy wonder why she'd spread her legs for him in the first place. Well, it didn't matter anymore. She'd moved to Oregon going on twelve years now, and that was one state Luke had no intention of ever visiting.

"Hey." Annie laid a hand on his arm. The sweet warmth of her touch melted the tension building in the back of his neck and shoulders. "Let's talk about something else."

"Good idea." He picked her hand up and kissed the back of it. "We have much better things to do."

Laughing softly, she leaned into him.

Today was all about Annie. Tomorrow he'd go after Seabrook to settle things once and for all. He was damn tired of other people running his life.

10

ANNIE MOVED CLOSER to Luke. A catch in her throat prevented her from speaking, though there really wasn't anything to say. Nothing needed to be said. Luke understood her fears, her yearnings, her shame. It was in his gentle kiss, in the soothing stroke of his palm down her arm.

In the warm humid air, she shuddered. She couldn't help herself. Emotions floated frighteningly close to the surface, making her feel so vulnerable she wanted to run away screaming. She wanted to crawl into Luke's lap until she went numb. She wouldn't cry though. She never did that. Not since she was twelve and her mother hadn't shown up for yet another birthday. But she was close now. What a mess. If the guys from the precinct could see her like this...

"I know," Luke whispered into her ear, and that was almost her undoing.

She clung to him like a drowning woman, and in a way she *was* sinking into a whirlpool of pent-up emotions. But why now? Damn it. Not now. Please, not now.

"Let's go for a swim," Luke said softly. "The water's cold but it'll feel good."

She nodded, and he went to work unbuttoning her blouse and then he pushed it off her shoulders. She shook it free but, when he started to unhook her bra, she stopped him. Not missing a beat, he unfastened her cutoff jeans and pulled them off.

Sitting in only a black bra and black bikini panties, she thought about all the times she'd gone jogging when it was raining or snowing and she'd longed not to leave her warm bed. In this moment, with the appreciative look he was giving her, it made it all worth it. In broad daylight, too, with all her body's flaws in full view. The bullet scar, the ugly mole near her collarbone, the dimples on the side of her thighs that no diet or exercise could seem to erase.

Still, he stared at her as if she were the most beautiful creature on earth. Obviously that wasn't so, but he made her feel like it, right to the bottom of her toes. He made her feel incredibly special. At least that's what she thought this feeling was.

Kneeling beside her, he pulled up the hem of his T-shirt and then yanked it off, exposing his amazing chest. He had a couple of scars, too, slashing the side of his ribcage, but on him they looked good. So did the one on his right jaw. Rugged. Sexy. Like the models on posters and billboards.

He got to his feet and unsnapped his jeans. Very slowly, he pulled down his zipper. At first she thought he was teasing her, but then she realized his slow motion was precautionary. He was hard and pushing against the denim.

Her pulse speeding, she got to her knees to help him. By that time he was just about unzipped, so she tugged the jeans down his muscled legs and he stepped out of them. All that was left were his boxers. She looked up at him and their gazes locked. She wanted so badly to see him, to taste him, but he had every right to refuse. She'd stopped him from stripping her naked.

He pushed down the boxers himself and she smiled. How could she have forgotten for one second that he was a guy? Of course he wouldn't refuse. She helped him get the soft blue fabric down to his ankles, the proximity of his thick hard penis too close to her mouth for her to think about anything else. As soon as he kicked the boxers aside, she gave into temptation and touched him with the tip of her tongue.

His sharp intake of breath nearly threw her off balance, or maybe it was the tremor that shot through his body. He clutched her shoulders and, when she took his cock into her mouth, he groaned and his fingers dug into her skin. She didn't take him in deep, but licked and teased, enjoying the way his thigh muscles tensed and bunched beneath her palms.

"Annie." His voice broke. "Wait."

She ignored him, circling her tongue around the smooth slick heat.

He gripped both sides of her head but made no attempt to stop her. His body quivered and, when an unexpected breeze came off the lake, Annie shivered, too.

God, she was in only her underwear and he was naked. Yes, they were surrounded by trees, with hills to the south and west of them, but anyone could show up by car or on horseback and catch them in the act. How insane was this?

She moved back and looked up at him.

He opened his eyes and smiled. "Let's get in the water."

"Yeah."

He helped her to her feet and then reached around her to unhook her bra. This time she let him. It was only fair. Besides, the hungry way he looked at her pretty much had her tongue-tied. She did glance around though, to double-check that no one was watching. The only sign of life was a squirrel darting from one cypress tree to another.

Anxious to be hidden by the water, she quickly pulled down her panties and flung them on the blanket where Luke had tossed her bra. He took her hand and they walked the few yards to the waterline. She tried not to gawk at him, but it was really hard keeping her face forward.

How could he possibly have no imperfections other than a few scars? Not an ounce of fat, not even a hair in the wrong place.

"It's gonna be cold at first," he said. "Probably better to run in and get it over with."

She looked at him and her breath fled. He was huge, hard, ready. For her.

"Annie?"

She forced her gaze away.

"Ready?"

"Yep."

He tugged at her hand. "Let's go."

"Wait!" The water wasn't just cold, it was freezing. She would have backed out, but he held on to her and drew her along with him, laughing, although she didn't know what was so funny.

"Come on. Get in here!" He'd lowered himself so that the water hit him mid-chest. His gaze went to her breasts. "Or maybe not."

She splashed some water in his face, and he laughed. "What else is in here besides fish?" Not that she considered fish benign, but they were a known entity and she counted on them not getting too close, anyway.

"Nothing but a very horny man." He pulled her toward him and she went down to her chin.

She came up sputtering, and gave him a solid push that sent him backward into the freezing water. "I thought you were a lover, not a fighter."

She wiped the water from her face and waited for him to come up. But he didn't. She stepped closer and tried to peer into the blue-green depths but, between the shadows and the reflections of the tall pines, she couldn't see more than a few inches. Panic rose in her chest. She hadn't pushed him that hard. But there were rocks on the bottom and he could have easily hit his head…. "Luke!"

He emerged behind her, locking his arms around

her waist and hauling her up against him. His hands came up to cup her breasts. "Were you worried about me?" he whispered.

"You're a jerk." She briefly closed her eyes as he kneaded her breasts and teased her nipples, his strong chest cradling her back, making her feel oddly safe and invulnerable. Kind of like wearing a bulletproof vest on the job. The sense of security was more an illusion than a reality, yet reassuring enough that you could take the next step.

"Can't argue there."

"Don't say that." As nice as it was being cocooned in his arms, she turned around to face him. "You're not a jerk."

"You just said I was." He went straight for her nipples again.

"You know what I mean. You've made other similar self-defeating remarks and it's—"

Snorting, he lowered his hands. "Is this gonna end in a lecture?"

"I'm just saying—"

He stopped her with a savage kiss that made her lose her footing, but he was right there with his arms tightly around her, holding her steady. She slowly ran her palms up his chest and then back down until she felt him suck in his belly.

Lingering for a moment, knowing she was driving him crazy, she inched closer to his penis until the back of her hand lightly brushed him.

The cold water had taken some of the wind out of

his sail. Her nipples suffered the opposite effect. She slid her arms around his neck and rubbed the hard tips across his chest. He shuddered, and she did, too.

"Cold?" he asked, drawing his palms down her arms, and then taking her hands and bringing each one to his mouth for a kiss.

"Not really. But you seem to be having some issues."

His lips twisted in a wry smile. "Yeah, well, I forgot about the cold water factor."

It took her a second and then she laughed. "Maybe that's a good thing."

He drew back to look at her. "How could that be a good thing?"

"It'll force us to take things slower." She reached between them and touched the silky smooth head, and smiled when it twitched.

"Darlin', it's never over after the first ride. You know I can get right back on that bull."

She laughed. "I'm not sure I appreciate that metaphor."

Smiling, he ran his palms down her back and over the swell of her buttocks and then cupped her to him. "This is the part of you I like best."

She didn't understand until he started to knead her backside. "My butt?"

"Uh-huh." He kissed the top of her shoulder.

"Not my sparkling wit?"

"That, too."

"What about my keen intuition?"

Working his way down to her breasts, he smiled against her skin. "Yep."

"And excuse me, but you forgot—" She cut herself short when he raised his head.

"You're amazing in every way," he said, his serious eyes engaging hers.

She gave him a light shove. "I was only teasing."

"Look at you, smart…successful… Man, you got it together in spite of all that crap with your parents."

"What about you?" Heat crept into her cheeks. If he only knew the rage she sometimes felt, especially during the holidays. Yeah, Lisa's parents always included Annie. They were great. But it wasn't the same. In fact, watching them interact like a loving family sometimes made her feel worse. "You have your own fan club."

"I'm serious."

"So am I. You found something you love to do and you're doing it. And doing it well, from what I hear."

"Don't." He looked away and slapped at the water, sending a small wave toward shore. "Gotta be pretty stupid to keep getting on a bull you know is gonna throw you sooner or later."

She chuckled. "You don't fool me. You love it."

"Yeah," he said with a trace of sarcasm.

"Well, then why do you do it?"

"Money." He looked at her breasts, only partially covered by the water. "Maybe you're not so smart after all. We're standing here naked and you want to talk about—"

She reached down and grabbed a handful.

He jerked. "Hey, I may need those."

"Exactly." She started at the base of his penis and slowly stroked toward the head.

He closed his eyes, and murmured, "Man, is this humbling."

She smiled. "Why?"

"Don't play with me, darlin'."

"Oh?" She withdrew her hand and his eyes flew open.

"Hey, that's not what I meant."

Annie laughed. "You have to be more specific."

"Oh, yeah?" He grabbed both her wrists. "You want specific?"

"Yeah, I want specific," she said, lifting her chin in challenge. Problem was, he could probably feel her pulse racing.

He grinned, his eyes gleaming wickedly. "Can you swim?"

Was this a trick question? Should she admit she was on her college swim team? "Kind of."

"Can you float?"

"Why?"

He turned her around and slipped his arms under hers. Crossing his arms over her chest, he brought her snugly against him, gently kneading her breasts and kissing her neck and shoulders. He nipped her earlobe and then said, "Now lean back. I've got you."

She hesitated. "What are you going to do?"

"You'll like it. Trust me."

Annie took a deep breath. He could've asked her for anything else, but trust didn't come easy. "Okay," she said finally, and tried to relax.

He tugged her back, and she let her legs float to the top. "You okay?"

She smiled. "I know how to float on my back."

"Good." He let her go.

Wary of what he was up to and feeling too exposed, she almost dropped down, but he was suddenly at her side, running his gaze along the length of her body. When he touched the tip of each nipple and then trailed his finger down between her ribcage, to her navel, to the juncture of her thighs, she had to struggle to keep from sinking.

"You said I was going to like it," she reminded him. "Torture isn't at the top of my fun-things-to-do list."

"Then I guess I'd better speed things up." He moved toward her feet and took hold of her ankles to spread her legs apart.

"What are you doing?" She slapped at the water, afraid she really was going down this time.

"Relax." He placed her legs over his shoulders so that her butt barely touched the water, and then positioned his head between her thighs, his mission now clear.

She glanced around. A squirrel ran up the bark of a tree. Birds chirped loudly, but she couldn't actually see them. Being naked and submerged was one thing, but this… "Luke…"

"Shh. If anyone gets close we'll hear them."

Oh, this was crazy. She was a cop…if someone caught them…if they were arrested…

He stroked her tensed thighs with his mouth and chin. "Doesn't the water feel good? The hot sun on your face?" he asked in a low hypnotic voice. "Close your eyes, darlin' and you can be anywhere you want to be."

Taking a deep breath, she concentrated on relaxing, but lying there naked wasn't the least of it—his face was right *there*. And then she felt his fingers, probing, spreading her lips and doing *incredibly wonderful things* that stopped her from thinking about anything else.

He put one finger in her and then another. She jerked and had to move her arms to keep from going under. But she wouldn't have, because his other hand cupped the small of her back and she knew, for whatever insane reason, that he wouldn't let her sink.

He withdrew but, before she could suffer the loss, he put his mouth on her. Her eyes flew open and her muscles tensed. Not because it felt wrong, just the opposite. His talented tongue had found her clit and, as she relaxed more and more, the pleasure deepened.

She'd never been a huge fan of the whole cunnilingus thing, but clearly that was because she'd only had experience with rank amateurs. Luke's technique combined the softness of velvet with a hard, pointy tip for accuracy and pressure. She grinned without moving her head. It would look bad if she drowned naked, while trespassing. But jeez, could she stop the critical analysis for one minute?

Her eyes fluttered closed once more as she slowed her breathing and let her thoughts go where they would. Go figure, they went right between her legs.

To add to the stupefying effect of his tongue, he slipped his finger back inside her. Slowly, he moved it in then out, all while the tip of his tongue flicked her hard, then softer, then harder, a counterpoint to his thrusts. He didn't keep to any rhythm, which bothered her for about a tenth of a second, until she realized that keeping her guessing made everything more intense.

The boy had done this before.

She squirmed, and he kept her afloat. So she breathed slowly, again, zeroing in on feeling so good that it had to be illegal.

His finger was moving faster and so was his tongue, and surely she would drown if she came like this. Her muscles tensed again and her wiggles became more dangerous. His hand on her back reassured her, but no, if she let herself go, she would really drown.

Holding back wasn't in her nature. Holding back, when Luke McCall was doing whatever he was doing, wasn't possible.

So she'd drown. It was one hell of a way to go.

She opened her mouth as her whole body contracted with her orgasm. Just as the water reached her temples, Luke swooped her up in his arms, protecting her, at least from drowning. Not so safe from his kiss.

He tasted salty like the ocean, like sex. She shuddered as her breasts dipped under, at the languid swirl of her legs and hands.

He had her. He wouldn't let her go. She was safe, and she was happy and she couldn't remember the last time she'd felt this way.

They stayed like that for a long time. She floating, he just touching her where he could, kissing her as if she was his favorite flavor. When he moved his mouth to her breasts, she was cogent enough to let him know she wouldn't mind returning the favor. "We'd have to get out, though, because I'd kill us both."

"Hmm, let me think about that," he said. That was followed by a chuckle, and his warm breath on her breast. "Thanks anyway, darlin', but I'm exactly where I want to be."

"Really?"

"No ifs, ands or buts," he said, as his hand caressed her bottom.

"Cute," she said. "Very cute."

"Close your eyes, Annie," he whispered, his voice as sultry as the breeze. "Don't sweat it. I've got you."

She'd known the man for about thirty seconds but damn if she didn't believe him.

IT KILLED HIM to put an end to her pleasure, but if Luke didn't go back to the ranch now, he wouldn't get anything done. And he'd feel like an even bigger loser for not only leaving her without notice, but without a lot of the work completed. "Annie?"

She opened her eyes and blinked at him. "What happened?"

"Nothing bad. You fell asleep, that's all."

Her brow knitted as she looked down and found them both on the blanket, naked as the day they were born. Luke held back his grin, understanding her perplexed expression exactly. How many times had he awoken to find himself stark naked somewhere strange? He'd give her a minute to adjust.

As he watched her rub her eyes and push back a loose strand of hair, he wondered if it was such a bright idea to give and not receive. He'd wanted this to be a perfect memory for her, something she'd think about with a smile in years to come. Unfortunately, he'd underestimated Annie. He'd actually had to find his own release after she'd fallen asleep. Which is the only reason he was even able to remember work.

He wanted to get that damn porch fixed before he left. And if he could have, he would have stayed until the ranch was in top shape. He couldn't. Instead, all he knew was that, once it was over and his name was cleared, he'd find Annie again and apologize. She probably wouldn't care, but he would.

She tempted him with another look, but he grabbed his pants. As long as he didn't look at her, luscious curves and beauty combined, he'd be fine. Okay, so he couldn't think about her, either.

"Seabrook," he muttered, picturing the old bastard. That did the trick.

11

LUKE WOKE UP before Annie, and rolled onto his side to look at her. They'd slept late after going to bed well past midnight. Daylight already streamed in through the old-fashioned blue-checked curtains, lighting Annie's sun-streaked brown hair. The wild mass spread out over her pillow and spilled onto his. Her dark lashes lay on her cheeks and her peachy lips were slightly parted.

The sheet didn't quite cover one breast and it took all of his willpower not to take a taste. But she needed sleep and he needed to get ready to hit the road.

Okay, yes. He should have told her already. But how could he have ruined last night? They'd returned home, showered together, worked outside until dark, and then showered again and made love twice before exhaustion forced them to hit the pillows.

That he'd repaired the porch last night instead of blowing it off to crawl into bed with Annie surprised him. Guilt. That had been the motivation. He was going to be leaving her with an awful lot of work. With any luck, he'd get to Joanne tomorrow and make her realize that he would disappear so she didn't have to admit to their affair. Yeah, she might lose a few bucks if her husband gave her the boot, but Luke's reputation was on the line. Hell, the rest of his life.

He picked up a lock of Annie's hair and rubbed the strands between his fingers. The smell of her almond shampoo lingered on the linen and made him think of last night. Their shower. How he'd scrubbed her back, her hair. How she'd run her hands all over his wet body.

It still shocked him that he was able to have that repeat performance last night, yet here it was again. He hadn't been this hard this often for a lot of years. He reached for his cock and a burst of pain shot through his shoulder. Quickly, he rolled back and straightened his arm. The burning lessened, but not his anger.

When he'd pried the rotting boards from the porch he knew he'd hurt something. He'd even heard the click. But it hadn't hurt for most of the night, not like the way it burned now.

So here he was. He needed just one more win and he'd have that spread he wanted. If he didn't make it to Houston next month, they might as well lock him up. At least he'd get three squares a day.

He flexed his shoulder and thought about his ointment, and about how he didn't want to wake Annie, but he had to chance it. Driving to Fort Worth with the pain would be a bitch. Tyler's truck's steering wheel was tighter than a bull's ass.

Damn he missed his Corvette. Missed his sorry excuse for a life.

Slowly, Luke lifted the sheet from his body, wincing from the pain when he made a wrong move. His duffel bag was still in the other room, which would make it easier to pack and get dressed once he got out of bed. But lifting the sheet had also given him a good look at both of Annie's perfect pink-tipped breasts.

He hesitated, briefly considered staying in bed until she woke up. But his plan was a good one. Get dressed, packed, make coffee and, if she wasn't awake by then, he'd get her up. Tell her he had an emergency. That he'd be back as soon as he could. If he could. She wouldn't believe him about coming back, and at one time he'd been the kind of guy who made empty promises like that. Not now. Not with Annie. But he wouldn't be able to convince her otherwise and he sure wasn't looking forward to the conversation.

Luke slid out of bed and stopped for a last look at her sleeping. God, he liked this woman. No syrupy sweet talk. Plain speaking and to the point. Shame he was gonna have to say goodbye.

"WELL, HELLO, Sheriff, are you calling for me or my husband?"

Jethro quickly swallowed the hunk of glazed doughnut he'd just bitten off. He hadn't expected Joanne to answer. "Good mornin', ma'am, I'm actually looking for Mr. Seabrook."

"I'm hurt. I thought you'd be calling for me." Ice clinked in a glass.

Ten in the morning and she was already drinking. Could be orange juice, but he doubted it. "I'm still in Hasting's Corner."

"Okay, then you're forgiven, Jethro." Her throaty laugh stirred Little Jethro. Ice clinked again.

"Is Mr. Seabrook in?"

She sighed. "No, he left a half hour ago. How far is Hasting's Corner from here, anyway?"

He hoped that was an idle question since she wasn't from around these parts. "Near two hours." He almost asked why but decided not to open that door.

"I can give Ernest a message but I think he went to Amarillo, which means he won't be home for hours, at least not until late evening." She made a purring sound. "Guess I won't have anyone to rub suntan lotion on my back."

An image of Joanne in a tiny pink bikini flashed before him. The previous June, at the pool at Seabrook's ranch, Jethro had met Joanne for the first time, and he remembered thinking how he'd never seen a swimsuit that small before. Not on a real live person, anyway. Her breasts had barely been covered and, when she'd bent over to pick up her drink, he could see all the way to Mexico. Her nipples were large and more brown than pink. Since then, he'd pictured them in his mind a whole lot more than he should have.

He eyed the small black bag he'd brought with

him. It was already packed, sitting on the ugly orange motel chair. He was at a dead end. No sign of McCall, and no one in Hasting's Corner was talking. He didn't think people were protecting Luke. They simply hadn't seen him, and Jethro didn't see any reason to stick around. But heaven help him if he made a move without getting Seabrook's approval. If the man would only carry a cell phone...

Little Jethro had been standing at attention, distracting big Jethro. He cupped his hand over his fly and applied some pressure. Maybe it would serve the windbag right if Jethro spent the day with Joanne.

"Are you there, sugar?"

He moved his hand. "Yes, ma'am."

"You're really annoying me, you hear?"

"Ma'am?"

"How old are you?"

He frowned. "Forty-two."

"Well, since I'm only twenty-nine, it sounds rather silly you calling me ma'am, doesn't it? I thought we'd agreed on Joanne."

Right.

"Jethro?" Her voice lowered to the husky purr again. "Today would be a really good day for you to come calling."

He looked down at the paunch that had pushed his belt to the final notch. His hair had started thinning the year before. Obviously, he was no Luke McCall and he didn't have any money. So what was she up to?

Still, he wouldn't mind a piece of her. If he didn't think Seabrook would kill him if he found out.

Someone knocked and, figuring it was the maid, he opened the door. Definitely not the maid. Late twenties, tall, blond and wearing a mini skirt.

She smiled. "Sheriff Wilcox?"

He nodded.

"I heard you were looking for Luke McCall," she said and walked into his room.

ANNIE DIDN'T KNOW what time it was, but it had to be time to get up. It was light out, even with her eyes half closed she could tell that much. She really had to talk to her aunt about installing some blinds or a blackout shade. Though she doubted her aunt ever slept past six.

Yawning, Annie rolled over onto her side, and peered at the empty space beside her. Luke wasn't there. Only the dent in his pillow remained. She ran her hand over the sheets, which were cool, so he'd been up for a while. Why hadn't he woken her?

She was wide awake now, prompted by a gnawing feeling of dread. Which was stupid. Luke was probably in the kitchen making coffee or talking to Chester. In fact, she smelled coffee brewing, but she still got up and looked out the window. His truck wasn't there, but then she remembered he'd parked it in the barn again when they got back from the lake.

So why did the uneasy feeling persist? Was it her overactive cop's imagination? Because last night had been incredible. If anything, she should feel giddy, not paranoid. She had to stop. Right now. Learn to enjoy.

She went around the bed to the nightstand. The pad with the hospital's number was next to the phone. First she'd call Aunt Marjorie and then Lisa. She'd have to call the Captain, too, let him know she'd be taking off the entire week, after all. Just as she was about to pick up the receiver, the phone rang, scaring her.

It was Aunt Marjorie.

"I was just going to call you." Annie sat on the edge of the bed and gathered the sheet to cover her bare breasts. As if it mattered. "Are your test results in?"

"Not until late this afternoon. I was calling to see how you and Chester are doing?"

"Fine. Um—" Annie had to stop and think. Hadn't she told Aunt Marjorie about Luke? Maybe not.

"Something wrong?"

"No, nothing. Do you remember a Luke McCall?"

"Heavens, yes. Did that boy finally come home?"

"Sort of. He's been helping Chester and me around the ranch."

After a long silence, she asked, "What's he doing with his granddad's place?"

"I have no idea."

"Suppose that's none of my business. But I do feel for the boy. That mama of his was hell-on-wheels and his old man never said a word in Luke's defense."

That *boy* snuck up behind Annie and cupped one of her breasts. She nearly squealed like a girl. Instead she swatted his hand away and pulled the sheets up tighter. "Tell you what, *Aunt Marjorie*," she said. "I'll call you later after your test results are in."

Annie said her goodbyes, hung up the phone and gave Luke a playful push.

He drew back as if offended. "Anyone ever tell you not to look a gift horse in the mouth?" He got a mug of coffee off the dresser where he'd left it and offered it to her.

"Okay, I forgive you." Black, just the way she liked it. She took a sip, set the mug on the nightstand and then she attacked.

She got him around the middle and, after a brief scuffle, they both ended up on the bed. Only he was fully dressed, and she wasn't.

"All right, darlin'," he said, capturing a wrist in each of his large hands. "You just remember who started this."

"Hey, wait."

"Better keep it down," he whispered. "Chester's in the kitchen."

"Okay." She struggled to get free but he ignored her, even when she hissed at him, and he drew her arms over her head exposing both breasts.

He gazed down at them for a few moments and then lowered his head and swirled his tongue around her right nipple. She tried to shrink away from him, but her body responded by arching to give him exactly what he wanted.

As if she didn't yearn for the same thing. With every breath she took she wanted him again. Inside her. Now. But with Chester in the house, that wasn't going to happen.

He threw one leg over and straddled her, then gently used his teeth to tease one nipple and then the other. Through his thick jeans she felt him getting hard against her belly. Moving her hips she wiggled into a better position, and smiled when she heard him groan. Using the distraction, she lifted her head and caught one of his shirt buttons between her teeth. She found the thread and, with one short jerk, the button came off. She had to spit it out before she swallowed the damn thing.

He looked up, mischief in his blue eyes. "You little witch."

She grinned. "Come on, let me up. I've got to get dressed."

"When I say you can."

She tried to knee him. Lightly, just enough to show him who was in control, but he dodged her. "Screw that."

"See, darlin', we're on the same wavelength."

She shook her head in mock annoyance. "If I yell, Chester will come running."

"You won't."

"Bet me."

He laughed and, to her disappointment, he let go and got off. "Later, we'll—" He blinked and the oddest expression crossed his face. Then he turned away so abruptly that her stomach clenched.

"Is anything wrong?"

"No, I, uh… I'm cooking breakfast." He smiled, but not his normal cocky grin. It was kind of a sad smile. "You got a preference?"

She shook her head, her gaze going to his chest. "Sorry about the button."

"No problem." He looked down and then started releasing the rest of the buttons.

"I'd offer to sew it back on but I think we'd have an even bigger mess."

His old grin was back. "Don't you fret, darlin'. I know how to sew on a button. Now, breakfast…I'm not sure how that's gonna turn out."

"Nice try." She pulled the sheet from the bed and wrapped it around herself before getting to her feet. "You offered. You're cooking. And by the way, I do have a preference. Eggs Benedict would be nice."

He frowned. "Eggs what?"

She laughed as she passed him, and then scooted when he tried to swat her bottom.

"Hey."

"What?" She clutched the sheet to her breasts and stayed a safe distance.

"Come here."

She didn't know which thrilled her more, the husky tone of his voice or the mock-dangerous look in his eyes, which made it difficult to keep a straight face. "Why?"

"Come here and I'll show you."

"Right." She backed toward the bathroom. "You go cook. Show and tell comes later tonight."

His smile didn't reach his eyes. "Sure."

Something was definitely wrong. As a cop, she was reasonably certain. As a woman, she didn't have a single doubt.

ON HIS WAY to the kitchen, Luke made sure the guest room door was closed. No sense in letting Annie see his packed bag before he had to tell her he was leaving. He'd wait till she was finished eating and then he'd talk to her. He'd have to hit the road right after that and get as far away from here as possible, yet stay in the county. Where? He hadn't figured that part out.

That thought made him look out the kitchen window. No strange cars in sight. But that didn't mean one of those bullheaded women wouldn't show up again.

Chester sat at the table, nursing a mug of coffee with all that junk he put in it. He didn't ask what had taken Luke so long, but of course Luke wouldn't expect that of him, either.

"I forget, Chester. How do you like your eggs?"

"Already ate." He didn't look up.

Luke sighed. "You gonna tell me what's wrong, or sulk all day?"

"I have one question and I want a simple answer." Chester put down the mug and looked Luke straight in the eye. "Are you leading that young lady on?"

He grinned on his way to the refrigerator. He and Annie both knew it was just sex but he couldn't tell

Chester something like that. "Actually, I was kinda thinking she might be leading me on."

Chester slapped his hand on the table. "Dang it, I'm serious."

"Calm down." He forgot about the eggs and bacon, and went to sit across the table from Chester. "Annie's a big girl."

"She's had enough trouble in her life. Ain't right for you to cause her any grief."

"Yeah, well, things are tough all over."

Chester briefly eyed him. "Thought you'd made peace with the past."

"I have. So has Annie."

The old man leaned back and stared with curiosity. "She told you about her pop?"

Luke nodded. "And her mother."

Chester frowned and looked off into space. "I ain't even had the guts to ask her about it. Her pop's out of prison then?"

Prison? Luke's chest tightened. What a freaking mess that must be; her a cop, her old man a criminal. She had to be downright humiliated. No wonder she hadn't mentioned it. He hadn't gone into any details about his family, either. For the same reason.

After too long a silence, Chester leaned forward and put his elbows on the table. His face was dark and accusing. "She didn't tell you about her pop?"

"She left the prison part out."

Chester cursed. It was only the second time Luke had heard a foul word out of the old man. The disappointment that entered Chester's eyes grew as he got to his feet. "I thought you'd changed, son."

Hurt and anger knotted Luke's gut. Chester had been one of the few people who'd given him the benefit of the doubt. The man hadn't once treated Luke like a loser. "You want me to leave? Fine. Today too soon?"

The old man had limped to the door. He hesitated with his hand on the knob. "I didn't say that."

Luke didn't care. Chester had given him an easy out.

"Don't go getting hotheaded, Luke. I want you to think about what you're doing." Chester exhaled sharply and, wincing a little, rubbed the thigh of his bad leg. "Guess I shouldn't have said nothing. But I don't want to see that girl hurt anymore."

Upset for feeling guilty, Luke watched Chester move slowly across the gravel toward the barn. Luke wasn't doing anything to Annie she didn't want done. She knew this was a short-term deal. Hell, he doubted she wanted anything different. Chester didn't know what he was talking about.

Luke went to the refrigerator and jerked the door open. He got out the bowl of eggs that Chester must've gathered this morning. One of the eggs cracked when he set the bowl down on the counter too hard.

"Damn."

He stared at the mess. Did *everyone* in the county think he was a loser? He would've bet Granddad's ranch that Chester would've stuck up for him. Or at least not accuse him of taking advantage of Annie.

So what if he had a reputation with the ladies? Chester knew him better than that.

Right. Luke sighed. That was the problem. He had been a jerk in his younger days. But he'd changed, grown up. Screw Chester if he couldn't see that.

The cracked egg had leaked over the others and he rinsed them off and put them back in the fridge. He was going to tell Annie right away and then leave. He doubted she'd have any appetite after that. It wasn't going to be easy.

He heard the bathroom door close, and braced himself. Then he heard something else. Outside. Tires crunching the gravel. No. Just what he was trying to avoid. He peered out the kitchen window, using the curtains for cover. The white sedan didn't seem familiar. He waited until the car made the curve, and then got a good look at the driver.

Luke stepped back.

Not now.

12

As SHE LEFT the bedroom, Annie thought she heard someone knocking. She prayed it wasn't another parade of women for Luke. Where was he anyway?

She hurried down the hall, noticing that the door to the room where Luke kept his things was closed. No one ever seemed to go around to the front of the house, so she headed straight for the kitchen door.

Through the screen she saw a man standing there, his fist in midair about to knock again. He was tall, thick around the middle and wore a black Stetson that hid half his face. He saw her, lowered his arm and tipped his hat. His smile was brief and businesslike, and when she opened the door, she saw the badge clipped to his belt.

"Mornin', ma'am."

"What can I do for you?"

He pulled the badge off his belt and held it up for her to see. "I'm Sheriff Wilcox. I was hoping you could give me some information."

"If I can."

"I'm looking for a man. Luke McCall's his name."

Annie stared at the sheriff. Speechless. Her stomach lurched, her hand automatically going there. What the hell had Luke done? She couldn't ask. Curiosity would give her away. Did she even want to protect him? Of course, just because the sheriff was asking about him didn't mean he'd done anything wrong. Maybe he'd inadvertently witnessed something. It could be…anything…like something really bad.

Oh, God.

Sheriff Wilcox stared back, his keen dark eyes assessing her reaction.

She silently cleared her throat. She could tell him she was a cop, but that would involve her on a whole new level. She needed time to find out what this was about before she volunteered any information about Luke or herself. "Maybe if you describe him. I don't know many people around here." She smiled. "I'm only visiting my aunt for a few days."

A sly, knowing grin curved the man's mouth, as if he knew she was lying. She'd used the same look herself to unnerve suspects. "Maybe your aunt has seen him," he said politely. "May I speak to her?"

"No, you can't." She paused, waiting for annoyance, or anything, to cross his face, but he stayed perfectly calm. Almost patronizing. But she didn't miss his attempt to furtively look past her into the kitchen. "She's in the hospital."

He nodded slowly. "Sorry to hear that, ma'am." He removed his hat and pushed his fingers through his thinning brown hair. "Sure is hot this mornin'. Might I trouble you for a glass of cold water?"

She knew what he was up to, but to refuse meant she might as well lead him right to Luke. "Certainly." She gave the screen door an extra shove to give him entry and turned back inside, knowing he'd follow.

Not that she could do anything about it, but she scanned the room, looking for evidence that indicated there was more than one person in the house. She saw it. Two mugs sitting on the counter near the sink, one still had coffee in it. He'd see them, too.

She got a glass out of the cupboard and then casually turned to catch his reaction to the mugs. He saw them all right. She could picture the wheels turning in his head. Maybe she ought to tell him she was a cop. Probably better to wait, in case things went south.

"Would you like some ice for your water?" she asked pleasantly.

"That would be real nice."

"Have a seat, and tell me about this man you're looking for." She lingered, running the kitchen tap and, while she had her back to him, she asked, "What did he do, anyway?"

Sheriff Wilcox was too smart for that. He waited until she turned around. "Stole a million dollars."

"Wow!" Oddly, relief surged through her. Luke obviously hadn't stolen a million dollars. Not with the truck he drove. Or the fact that he was working for her for room and board. She poured the sheriff's ice water, her hand shaking slightly. Fortunately, not enough for him to notice. "And you think this guy would still be hanging around with that kind of money?"

She looked over at him and caught his annoyed wince.

He met her eyes and smiled. "Have to cover all the bases, ma'am."

Before she joined him at the table, she purposely grabbed the mug still on the counter, filled it with coffee and brought it to the table with her.

His gaze went to the other mug. "I hope I'm not interrupting anything."

"Not at all. You're saving me from painting." She smiled. "Chester's already out doing his chores."

"Chester?"

"He's the one and only ranch hand. He's been with my aunt for over fifty years."

"I'd like to speak with him if I may."

"Sure." She checked her watch. "If you come back later this afternoon. He's out in one of the pastures doing whatever he does until then."

He nodded, his gaze going to the window, and then to her, giving her a quick once-over, before thoughtfully sipping his water. He should have been more interested in talking to Chester. What was he thinking?

"So tell me what this guy, Luke—" She waited until she had his attention. "What does he look like?"

That patronizing smile again. "Tall, maybe six-two, muscular, kind of dirty-blond hair, blue eyes. A real ladies' man, so I hear."

She laughed, the sound tinny to her ears. That was Luke, all right. "I think I'd remember a man like that." She paused. "Wait a minute. Someone did stop by looking for work. It was the day after I got here. He was tall, but if he'd stolen a million bucks, I'd doubt he needed work."

Sheriff Wilcox smiled. "Did he give you a name?"

"I don't remember."

"Did he say which way he was headed?"

"I only spoke to him for a minute."

The sheriff's cell phone rang. He excused himself and stepped outside to talk. Annie stayed where she was, even though she was dying to run down the hall and scream at Luke. Where was he? Who was he? What had he done? How desperate was he? He had said he needed money....

She watched the sheriff pace as he talked. He knew that she was hiding something. She wondered how far he was willing to push for the truth. He might ask to look around the house. Of course, she couldn't let him. But then again, if Luke was innocent, he could straighten everything out right now. Otherwise, it was her duty to give him up.

Her stomach knotted at the thought. Her chest and throat got so tight she wanted to be sick. The man had just been in her bed. He'd lied to her from day one. Sighing, she sank back in her chair. Chester and Aunt Marjorie had, in effect, vouched for him. But this sheriff... She didn't know him at all. He wouldn't be the first lawman to have a personal agenda.

Her thoughts kept racing, no matter how much she told herself to calm down. She had to think. Focus. Not react. She had to give Luke a chance to explain. She'd done well listening to her instincts and they told her to trust Luke.

"Sorry for the interruption, ma'am."

Damn, she hadn't heard him come back inside. "My name's Annie, not ma'am," she said crossly.

"That's a real pretty name."

"Look, I don't see how I can help you," she said quickly when he started to reclaim his chair. "Seems silly to waste your time."

"I'll finish my water, if you don't mind, and then I'll be off."

She almost told him to take the glass with him. "I don't mind at all." She took a sip of her coffee. "Is it always this hot at this time of year?"

"Mostly." He studied her closely, his gaze dropping to her red tank top. Even though she was braless, she knew it wasn't a sexual interest. "Mind if I poke around the barn?"

"What for?"

"Never can tell. McCall might be hiding out there."

She laughed. "Then Chester would've run him off with a shotgun."

"Just the same, I'd feel better if—"

She shook her head. "Can't let you do that."

He didn't seem surprised. "Why not?"

"If this were my place, I wouldn't have a problem with it. But I can't speak for my aunt."

He slowly nodded. "Well, then, I best be going." He took a final gulp as he got to his feet. "But I want to caution you to be careful if he shows up."

"Is he dangerous?"

"For the ladies. That boy can sweet talk the panties off a nun." He gave her a sheepish smile that she didn't believe for a minute. "Pardon my language."

No need to react. She already knew about that particular quality. "I'm from New York. I've met a few of those kind before, so you don't have to worry, Sheriff." She got to her feet to give him a hint.

"I hope not." His eyes probed hers. "A pretty lady like yourself would be the type he'd want to con."

Her heart sank. She tried to keep her face expressionless, to not let him see how his words had sliced her to the bone. All she wanted right now was for Sheriff Wilcox to get out of her aunt's house and leave her to deal with Luke in her own way.

"I'm going to give you my card with my cell number." He withdrew a card from his breast pocket and presented it to her. "If he shows up, or if there's anything you forgot to tell me, call anytime. Or, if you think you're in trouble," he said, his gaze locking on hers, "I won't be far."

She took the card from him and forced a smile. "Will do." No matter what he said, this guy wasn't going anywhere. He'd be sticking close. "Don't worry about me, Sheriff. I'm a police officer, too. Back in New York. I'm a sergeant, about to make detective. I assure you I can take care of myself." She threw the small lie about the promotion to detective in for good measure.

Brief surprise flickered in his eyes. But nothing else. "That a fact?"

Maybe he didn't believe her. More likely he was wondering why she'd withheld the information. Okay, she wasn't thinking straight. It would've been better to keep her mouth shut. "I'd have said something earlier, but I'm on vacation. I haven't had one in years, and I—" She sighed dramatically. "I'm leaving in a couple of days to go home, so I'm afraid I won't be much help to you."

"I understand." He hesitated, and this time he seemed to have genuine concern in his eyes. "Be careful, Sergeant. This guy's a real cool character. You may be a peace officer, but you're still a woman." She was about to object, but he added, "He slept with a judge once, and she dismissed the reckless driving charge against him."

Annie couldn't breathe. "Thanks, Sheriff, I'll keep that in mind."

He started to go and then turned, and frowned. "Did I tell you how he got to the money?"

She shook her head. She didn't care. She wanted Wilcox gone.

"He slept with a man's wife to gain access to their house. I thought you should know." He tipped his hat to her. "Thank you for your time and the water."

"No problem." She walked him to the door. "I wish you luck."

He gave her an annoyingly sympathetic smile and then headed for his car.

Her knees weak, she clung to the door and watched him until she could only see his brake lights. It took a few minutes before she could move, before she could trust herself to walk without her knees buckling. Then she only made it to the kitchen table.

Luke had used her. Just like her father had. Just like Steve. The son of a bitch had used her.

LUKE THOUGHT he heard the car leave, but he wasn't sure enough to move from the room. At least he could finally breathe. Annie hadn't given him up. She'd trusted him enough to hear his side. Not many people would do that. Not for him. Sure some of the local women might have protected him, but there would've been a price.

He stayed where he was, sitting on the edge of the narrow twin bed, waiting for Annie to come get him. It wasn't something he was looking forward to but he had a lot of explaining to do. What really killed him was that he couldn't hear what Wilcox had told her. He could only imagine what kind of tall tales the sheriff had described or scare tactics he'd used. Wilcox wasn't a bad guy, from what Luke knew of him, but he was scared of Seabrook and jumped at his every command. And that made Sheriff Wilcox dangerous.

Luke checked his watch. With the door and window closed and the sun beating down from the southeast, the small room was hotter than blazes. He supposed he could sneak out the window and see if the car was gone. But then if he got caught…

A knock at the door took the decision out of his hands. He stood, ready for action, and then he heard Annie say, "It's me." She opened the door and the devastated look on her face said it all.

"I should have told you." He moved toward her and, without a word, she turned around and walked down the hall to the kitchen.

She went straight for the window, staring blankly.

"Thanks for not turning me in." Luke took a chair and she the opposite one.

She wouldn't look at him, her hazel eyes darker than he'd ever seen them. A couple of red blotches marred the side of her neck. They sat in silence, Annie looking as if she'd been run over by a truck, while Luke kicked himself for being so stupid. He was everything everyone had ever said about him. Nothing but a loser. His old lady was right after all. That's all he'd ever be.

"What did he tell you?" he asked finally.

She did look at him then, her expression one of total disbelief, and then she shook her head. "How about you give me your version?"

"First of all, I didn't steal a thing. You have to believe that."

Her eyebrows arched, but she stayed silent. Okay, she was angry, and he didn't blame her. He just hoped he hadn't totally screwed things up with her.

"There's this guy, Ernest Seabrook. He owns half

the county, including the sheriff. He's also president of the stockmen's association. Those are the guys that put up prize money for the rodeos. Anyway, he's the one claiming I stole the prize money from his safe."

"Why would he do that?"

"There's been bad blood between us for a few years now." How he did not want to tell her about Joanne. "Maybe he took the money himself and wants to frame me."

"Were you ever at his home?"

"Once."

"Why?"

He hesitated, although Wilcox had probably already told her about Joanne. "I was visiting his wife."

"Visiting, huh?" She looked upset. "I suggest you tell me everything. Your credibility is already questionable. And that's being charitable."

"Okay, okay." Luke sighed. This wasn't going well. "Seabrook's wife and I had an affair."

"Really?" She tried not to show it, but she was hurt. Anger would have been better. He could deal with that. "Funny, I seem to remember you saying something about never sleeping with married women. Shameful I think was the word you used. Guess that was all bull. For my benefit, no doubt."

"No, that's not true. I meant what I said. Joanne was a mistake. I didn't know she was married."

"Right. You know this guy well enough that there's bad blood between you, and you go to his house, but you don't know that this woman is his wife."

"She told me she was his daughter."

Annie laughed humorlessly. "This is getting better and better."

"They hadn't been married long, just a few months, and she's half his age. I assumed she was his daughter, who'd come home from school or back from Europe, and she didn't set me straight. Because he didn't like me, we had to sneak around. I didn't question that. And yeah, I admit I got off on sticking it to the old bastard by sleeping with his daughter. But I also liked Joanne. Before I found out she'd lied."

Annie stared at him, her lips parted in amazement. And then she shook her head, looking so sad it made his chest tight. "So you know what it feels like to be lied to by someone you like."

"I didn't lie exactly," he said. "I didn't tell you the entire truth."

Anger replaced the sadness in her eyes. "How is that different?"

"Look, Annie, I didn't mean to hurt you."

She made a strangled sound that tore at him. "You used me."

"No, no." Luke briefly closed his eyes. That was the last thing he wanted her to think. "I didn't. I wanted to protect you. In fact, I was planning on leaving this morning. I'm already packed. Go see for yourself."

Her expression crumpled. She looked at him as if he were the lowliest critter on earth.

"I'd decided to tell you at first. Right after breakfast."

"Gee, that would have made it better."

"Annie—"

"You weren't trying to protect me. You were leaving to save your ass."

"That, too. I admit it." He wasn't getting through to her. He wasn't sure he knew how to. In the past, when things got rough, he left. Maybe that was what he should do now. Leave. Get the hell out of her life. But first, he had to make her understand. "I swear to God, I never wanted you involved in all this."

"How can you say that? You used me to hide out."

"I never thought it would come to this. I needed a safe place, and you needed someone to do some work around here."

"Oh, please. I was the perfect mark. Not only a woman, but a cop, too. You must've had a damn orgasm when you found out."

He laughed at that, but then could tell she wasn't trying to be funny. "Are you kidding? It scared me. I had to have time to prove that I'm being framed, not worry about whether you were looking over my shoulder."

She blinked, looking unsure, and then stared him straight in the eye. "Did you steal that money?"

He held her gaze steady. "No."

"Did you sleep with a judge to make a reckless driving charge go away?"

"Fuck." He slumped back.

"I'll take that as a yes."

"I was twenty-four at the time, and she came on to me."

Amazingly, she didn't look totally disgusted. She leaned back in the chair, her eyebrows all puckered as if she was thinking really hard.

"Look," he said, "I don't know what else Wilcox told you, but I was no saint as a kid. I made some mistakes. No, I made a lot of mistakes. When I was young, in my teens and early twenties, I did whatever I had to do to get by. That's not an excuse, but I'm a different man now."

"Why do you think this guy's framing you?"

Luke rubbed his forehead. What a time to have a headache the size of Texas. "At first, I figured the money wasn't actually missing, but that this was a good way for him to give me a hard time because of Joanne and me. If he keeps me on the run and I can't ride in the Houston rodeo, that's gonna hurt."

"But the money has to be missing if he's gotten the law involved."

Luke snorted. "Wilcox is in debt up to his eyeballs to Seabrook. I'm not sure he has much of a choice but to listen to him. The fact that the so-called theft hasn't been made public is another reason I think this is a ruse. But then again, there's Seabrook's pride. He wouldn't want everyone in the county knowing about me and Joanne."

Sighing wearily, Annie put her elbows on the table and tightly folded her hands in front of her. She leaned forward slightly and pinned him with a stern stare. "I'll help you, but if you're lying about one damn—"

"Thank you, Annie." He reached for her hands.

She withdrew, lowering her arms to her sides. "Better that you don't touch me anymore."

13

ANNIE NEEDED a drink. She didn't imbibe often, but neither did she make it a habit to aid and abet a criminal. Only eleven-ten. The hell with it. She got up from the table and went to the cupboard that held a bottle of brandy. She got out a small glass, then hesitated, trying to decide whether to offer Luke any. She was still so mad at him she could strangle him. But then, some booze might loosen him up, prompt him to tell her anything he might've left out.

She was totally insane for helping him. Although, after incriminating herself with Wilcox, she had a vested interest in the outcome. What made her furious was that she hadn't simply been a foolish, gullible woman—she was human, she'd allow herself the flaw—but she'd been a lousy cop. Up until now, that had been the one thing she'd done right in her life. What had she been thinking?

God, what was it going to take for her to learn? How could she have thought for one moment that Luke had been interested in her, when he could have his pick of women. She poured half a glass of brandy and took a gulp. The liquid burned all the way down to her empty belly. They'd skipped dinner last night because they'd been too anxious to get under the covers.

Oh, God. She took another gulp.

"Annie?"

She looked over at him. He had the nerve to look concerned. Screw him. She poured another half glass and carried it and the bottle to the table. Luke got up and got his own glass. His well-worn jeans hugged his lean hips and perfect ass. His hands still fascinated her, so large and strong, but gentle enough they'd brought her body to life.

Watching him made her want to weep. She took another sip instead, knowing this would be the last of the brandy for her. She needed to keep a clear head and stay unemotional. Tough enough to be un-biased, as it was.

He sat down, took the bottle and poured a very small amount, but then swallowed it in one gulp. He pushed both the bottle and glass away. "Does Chester know?"

"Not that I'm aware of. Sheriff Wilcox drove straight out the driveway. But frankly, I don't think he needed to talk to anyone else. He knew you were here."

Luke muttered a curse under his breath. "As soon as Billy saw me, I should have left." He stared down at a particularly bad gouge in the oak table and traced it with his finger. When he looked up again, his eyes were full of regret. "I'm so sorry, Annie. I know I've put you in a terrible spot. Maybe you should turn me in."

"Maybe I should."

"I wouldn't blame you one bit."

"I wouldn't care if you did."

"I know," he said quietly.

Sighing, she rotated her neck, trying to get rid of the tension. Her stomach burned, probably from the brandy. "All right, let's start at the beginning."

He snorted. "Which beginning?"

Her temper sparked again. "If you're not going to cooperate—"

"It's not that— Seabrook and I go way back. I've never liked the way he's treated his animals and I was outspoken about it. That started the friction between us, about seven years ago."

"Okay, and I assume you've crossed paths since."

"We've pretty much stayed clear of each other. Besides, he's too uppity to hang around with cowboys."

It occurred to her that she should be taking notes, so she got up to search for the pad of paper. "When did you meet Joanne?"

He muttered something unintelligible. Clearly he didn't want to talk about her. Tough. Annie didn't, either. If he hadn't been so quick to unzip his fly, they'd be doing something far more enjoyable than trying to keep his perfectly delectable ass out of prison.

She found a small spiral notebook and a pencil in the drawer near the brown wall phone. When she returned to the table, he was sitting with his eyes closed and pinching the bridge of his nose. The sound of her chair legs scraping the linoleum made him open his eyes.

"Ready?" she asked, the pencil poised.

He stared at it as if it were a weapon. "What are you doing?"

"I need to keep a chronological list of events to keep me straight."

He slowly nodded. "Yeah, okay. How much does Chester have to know about this?"

"Good point. Since Sheriff Wilcox has been here and made it known that you're wanted, Chester has to decide if he's in or out. If he's in, and you're caught here, we're all accomplices after the fact."

"Please. I can't do this to Chester and you. Find a handyman in town to help with the repairs." He got up. "I put you in this predicament so I'll pay for it."

Annie glared at him.

"Yes, I have money, and no I didn't steal it."

"Sit down."

"If I leave now, Wilcox will never have to know I was here and y'all are in the clear."

"Number one, there are enough witnesses who can put you here, so that ship has sailed. Second, I lied for you. I'll never be in the clear. Now, sit down."

The stricken look on his face as he lowered himself back into the chair almost got to her. But slick as he was, how did she know it wasn't an act?

"Annie—"

She closed her eyes. "Don't."

They sat in silence for several moments and, after Annie pulled herself together, she looked at the blank paper in front of her.

He automatically started talking, describing everything from the first time he'd met Joanne and how he'd been led to believe she was Seabrook's daughter. He didn't stop until the night he picked Annie up on the side of the road.

Some of it was hard to hear, especially his and Joanne's sneaking around. Annie carefully kept her eyes on the growing list of events. Objectivity was difficult. Her thoughts kept going to bad places. But, bottom line, she was a cop. A good one. She could do this. She hoped.

SHERIFF WILCOX parked on the side of the road under the shade of a juniper and behind some scrub oak. From this vantage point he had an excellent view of the beginning of the driveway. No one could come or go without him seeing them. Cop or not, that woman was hiding something.

Well, he'd likely have a long wait and he had no coffee or cold soda, only a warm bottle of water. And still he hadn't heard from Seabrook. Probably just as well. Jethro wouldn't be going anywhere for a while. Still, it would be nice to give the old man good news for a change.

Sighing, he opened all four windows. Around here there weren't as many mosquitoes, but the sun was still hot enough to bake him like a chocolate cake.

Which reminded him… He leaned over and opened the glove box. A map and the magnifying glass he used for the fine print fell out. He stuck his hand in and rooted around until he found it. He pulled out his emergency chocolate bar, so melted from the heat that with one small tear of the wrapper, the chocolate oozed onto his fingers.

He was licking it off when his cell phone rang. Hastening to answer it, the slim phone slid from his slippery fingers. Quickly he cleaned his palm on the front of his jeans and recovered the phone.

"Jethro? It's Joanne."

"Ma'am?"

She clucked her tongue impatiently. "Joanne Seabrook."

He smiled, keeping his eyes on the driveway entrance. "You heard from your husband?"

"That's why I'm calling. Looks like he'll be spending the night in Amarillo."

"That a fact? He leave a number where I can reach him?"

She made a most unladylike sound. "Jethro Wilcox, you can be so obtuse sometimes."

He didn't know why he liked baiting her so much. Maybe it was because she was Seabrook's property and Jethro knew, no matter how much she offered it up, he couldn't go for it. "Thing is, ma'am, I think I found McCall."

A soft gasp, and then, "Where?"

"Near Hasting's Corner."

"Have you actually seen him?"

"No, but I'd bet my badge I'll have him by tomorrow." After the silence lasted too long, he added, "That's why it's important I speak to Mr. Seabrook."

"Well, he's working on some big deal," she muttered, her distraction obvious. "Since he's staying the night, he'll call and tell me what hotel he's at. This isn't good," she whispered, as if to herself.

"What's not good?"

"What? Oh, um, it's delicate, Jethro. I'm not sure how to explain."

"Don't you worry. I've heard it all, ma'am. If it's pertinent to the case, it's best you tell me."

She sighed. "Luke didn't steal the money. No one did. Ernest thinks I was having an affair with Luke and he wants to punish him."

Jethro had already figured out half of that, himself. The money part he wasn't sure about. "If that's the case, I'd imagine your husband will drop the charges before it goes any further."

"What if he doesn't?"

"Pardon my saying so, ma'am, but Mr. Seabrook doesn't strike me as a man who'd want the whole county to know his wife was cheating on him."

"I didn't say I actually had an affair with Luke."

"No, ma'am, you didn't."

Joanne paused. "All right, so I had a small slip in judgment. Should Luke and I both have to pay for it for the rest of our lives?"

A maroon pickup was coming from the other

direction, but it didn't slow down and passed the driveway. Jethro took a good look as it passed him. Inside, there were a couple of teenagers who paid him no attention. "I'm not following you."

"Luke will go through anything to prove he's innocent. As for me, that's obvious. Ernest will have to divorce me. As you pointed out, he has too much pride to ignore this tiny indiscretion."

"But you think he knows."

"I'm fairly certain. I think one of our maids, who totally hates me and spies on me every chance she gets, has been filling his ear with all kinds of nasty things about me."

Jethro smiled. "None of them true, right?"

After a brief silence, "Are you making fun of me, Sheriff?"

He chuckled. "Sorry."

"That's all right. I was starting to think you had no personality at all." Her laugh was sexy and throaty, and he could pretty much guess what was coming next. "I was thinking that if you bring Luke to me, instead of to Ernest, that you and I might be able to get to the bottom of this."

"I'm not taking him to anyone, ma'am. I'm just bringing him in, period."

"Come on, Sheriff, I know you're doing this on your own time and that Ernest is paying you privately. Maybe I presented this deal wrong. If you bring Luke to me, I'll make it worth your while."

Tempted to ask if she meant money or sex, he let

the remark slide, since it didn't matter. Seabrook was paying him a small fortune, and Jethro needed every penny. "I have to go. We'll talk later."

"Don't do anything until then, you hear?"

"Yes, ma'am." He severed the connection and went back to salvaging his chocolate bar.

Not even two minutes later, his cell rang again.

"Jethro?"

He groaned. It was his ex-wife, the second Mrs. Wilcox, wanting more money, no doubt. And while child support was one thing—he never resented a penny of that—the alimony bothered him good and plenty. It also kept him in the goddamn poorhouse.

LUKE WATCHED ANNIE take her time with her notes. In his whole life, he couldn't recall ever feeling so bad. Even his head and body ached as if he were hung over. Could guilt and shame do that? "There's something else I should probably tell you."

She looked up, her hazel eyes now a warm golden color. Man, she was pretty. Her hair was still kind of messed up, as if she hadn't brushed it since getting out of bed.

"I bought a gun."

She blinked and tilted her head to the side as if she hadn't heard right. "You have a gun?"

He nodded.

"What for?"

"I haven't been getting anywhere with Joanne so I figured I might have to face Seabrook himself."

"And a gun would help you do that?"

"I sure as hell wasn't gonna break into his estate without one."

"Break in." Annie shook her head. "Don't think anymore, okay. It's too dangerous."

"Funny."

"Hardly. Where's the gun?"

"I only bought it yesterday. It's still in the truck. Hidden under the seat."

"Yeah, because nobody would look there. Brother." She briefly closed her eyes, and exhaled with a huff. "Dare I assume it was a legitimate purchase?"

"I paid cash."

"That's not what I meant."

Luke sighed. "I didn't exactly buy it from a gun store, if that's what you mean."

"Okay." She put up a hand. "I don't want to hear anymore. You'll have to hand it over."

"To who?"

"Me. I *am* a cop. At least for now," she muttered and quickly looked down at the notebook. Her pale face told him more than her stony expression.

God, he was such an ass. Too self-absorbed to consider how hiding out here would affect Annie. Or Chester, for that matter. "Chester."

She looked up again, her eyes widening.

"No."

"Yeah." Her gaze strayed to the window. "I'll talk to him."

"Nope. It's over. I can't involve him."

"Too late, buddy. You should've thought about that before you weaseled your way in here."

He winced. The woman sure didn't pull any punches. "It's not too late. He doesn't know anything. It's not like he was hiding me."

Her expression softened for the first time since she'd walked into the guest room and looked at him as if he was pond scum. "Do you honestly think Chester would rather see you arrested than help if he could?"

Luke shrugged. "He doesn't owe me anything."

She studied him long enough that he got uncomfortable and looked away. "Luke? This isn't about owing anybody. Chester cares about you."

Restless suddenly, he got up and went to the fridge, opened it and got out the pitcher of orange juice. He sure shouldn't have any more brandy. Annie didn't understand. He didn't mean anything to Chester. Him and Granddad had been cardplaying buddies. Luke was their gofer. The end.

"Oh, I see," Annie said in a smug voice, and he looked warily at her. "You're one of those guys who pushes anyone away who gets too close."

He poured orange juice into his empty brandy glass and then set the pitcher in front of her with a thud. "Don't try and analyze something you don't know anything about."

Hurt flickered in her eyes, and then she blinked, "You're right. Let's get back to work," she said, all business again. "You'd said you originally wanted to get to Joanne. Why?"

"Because she knows I was never alone in the house. I couldn't have possibly found the old man's study and then the safe and broken into it."

"She doesn't want to alibi you, because then she'd have to admit to the affair," Annie said to herself, as she wrote a note.

"Right."

"This woman would rather see you go to prison?"

"Than give up Seabrook's money? Yep, that would be Joanne."

"Nice crowd you hang out with," Annie muttered, and then quickly looked down, as if she'd regretted the snide remark. "So, at this point, we have to assume Joanne wouldn't alibi you anyway." She stopped and thought for a moment. "We also have to account for the possibility that the money is missing."

"But Seabrook's motive isn't theft."

"But maybe he knows who did steal it and he's protecting them."

Luke scoffed. "It would snow down here in July before Ernest Seabrook stuck his neck out for anyone."

"Okay, then we'll operate on the assumption that the money isn't missing and he's just trying to screw you."

"That's my guess."

"Have you thought about calling his bluff?"

"You mean like turning myself in?"

She nodded. "It'll all come out about you and Joanne, and she'd be forced to give a statement."

Luke laughed humorlessly. "You know how long it would take to clear everything up? They could hold me long enough that I'd miss the Houston rodeo next month and Seabrook would love that." Unconsciously, he tried to rotate his shoulder, but a staggering pain gripped him.

Annie frowned. "Will you be able to ride by then?"

"Yeah." He avoided her eyes and reached for the pitcher with his good arm.

"They can't hold you without cause."

"Darlin', you don't know Seabrook. Or the way the people in this county bow at his feet. The law will hold me until kingdom come, if that's what Seabrook wants."

She wrinkled her nose as she stared off, deep in thought. Finally, she looked at him and said, "I need to meet with Joanne."

"Are you crazy?"

"I can get to her. You can't."

"You don't need to get in any deeper."

She slumped back. "I'm already in over my head."

His cell phone rang and they immediately looked at each other. It didn't ring often, and Luke half expected it to be Sheriff Wilcox.

He checked the ID screen. What the hell? "I think it's Joanne."

14

ANNIE WATCHED him talk to Joanne. Unless he was one hell of an actor, he had no hidden feelings for the woman. Although his voice was smooth and persuasive, tension pulled at the corners of his mouth and banked anger darkened his eyes. Annie knew, because not even for a fraction of a second did he break eye contact with her.

The connection created a weird kind of intimacy that she couldn't afford. They weren't coconspirators or partners, they weren't even lovers anymore. She was stuck in this position, hoping to salvage her career.

And yes, damn it, she wanted to prove that Luke was innocent. In spite of all the crap he'd pulled, in spite of the fact that he'd used her, she wanted him to be innocent, if only to confirm that her instincts were still intact. That, when it came to men, she didn't have one bit of sense. Clearly, that was true personally, but she'd always been a good cop. She couldn't let that be taken from her.

Mesmerized by his gaze, she realized her concentration was slipping and she forced herself to focus on what he was saying. Not that she could garner much. He gave brief answers, and it almost killed her not to hear Joanne's side.

Fortunately, the conversation was short and, as soon as it ended, he said, "She wants to meet."

Annie could tell he was as surprised as she was. "What's changed?"

"She talked to Wilcox. He told her he knows where I am."

"Damn it." Annie lifted her hair off her neck and twisted it up. It was hot and humid, and her soaring blood pressure didn't help. "I got the feeling he'd been tipped off. Probably by one of your jilted girlfriends," she said, ignoring the annoyed look on Luke's face. "But I thought I might've planted some doubt." She let go of her hair.

Luke's gaze followed its fall around her shoulders and down over her breasts. When he finally met her eyes, she had to steel herself against the vulnerability and regret reflected there. "So what's the plan?"

"We're meeting in three hours."

"Good. That'll give us some time." She nodded absently, her mind racing. True, she couldn't wire him, but they could…

"Not much. It'll take almost two hours to get there."

"Where is this place?"

"The motel just across the county line where we used to go," he said, his gaze flickering away. "But we're meeting at the diner."

"Okay." It didn't matter to her where they met.

Even if it was in one of the rooms. Annie and he were through. She saw him shaking his head, his lips moving slightly as if he were talking to himself. "What? You think of something else?"

"Of all places for this to happen."

"At the motel?"

He looked at her, his eyes dark and haunted. "No, here. Home." He threw his head back, his eyes closed. "Man, if my mother were here… I've got to clear this up. Everyone will think—" He cut himself short, embarrassment creeping up his neck. He glanced briefly at her and passed a hand over his face. "I wonder what Joanne's up to."

Annie knew exactly what he was thinking. He didn't want everyone to think his mother was right about him. The anguish on his face tore at her heart— sap that she was. "Any chance she's setting you up?"

"No way. She wants all this kept quiet. In fact, I wouldn't be surprised if she wants to give me money to disappear."

"Really?"

He shrugged. "It's a possibility…."

Annie thought about that for a moment. Maybe she'd give Lisa a call and ask her to run a check on Joanne. Younger woman, older rich man, maybe Joanne had done this before. Even if she had, it could mean nothing, but it was worth the shot.

"We should get moving." She glanced at the clock as she got to her feet. "I'll have to find Chester and fill him in, in case Wilcox comes snooping around—"

"If Chester has any—"

"He won't." She smiled, probably for the first time since Sheriff Jethro Wilcox stepped foot through the door and turned her world upside down. No, it was after Luke's first lie that her life had started to fall apart. She simply hadn't known it then.

She took a deep breath and reminded herself she couldn't go there. She had to stay focused. "You'll have to get her to admit to the affair, to prove that's why you were in the house in the first place, and then get her to explain why she won't alibi you. Is there a place on the way we can buy a small recorder?"

Nodding, he got up and started clearing the table. "How close will the thing have to be to pick up her voice?"

"Depends on how good a recorder we can find." She pushed her fingers through her hair and got them caught in a tangle. She twisted it again and stuck it in the back of her T-shirt to keep the bulk away from her face. "That's going to be a problem. She'd probably notice if you kept it in your breast pocket."

"That's why I was thinking I could set it on the seat beside me."

She picked up the glasses he put on the counter and started washing them. When he gave her a funny look, she said, "I don't know how far the good sheriff is willing to go to find you, and I don't want to leave evidence that I had company."

"Ah. Good thinking." He grabbed the dish towel and started drying, his shoulder brushing hers as they worked. He'd used her shampoo and the unique almond scent tantalized her senses.

That wasn't all he'd used.

Sudden resentment swelled inside her. Everything had been going so well for the past three days...hell, it was her fault as much as his. She'd been stupid enough to believe—to trust that someone wanted her with no strings attached. Shame on her.

She finished the last glass and then put away the brandy and orange juice. "Any ideas on how to get you off this property without being seen?"

"Annie?" He touched her arm, and she did all she could to keep from jerking away. "Thank you."

"Don't thank me yet," she said, flatly. "You may still end up some lifer's bitch."

ANNIE WAITED in the car until Luke got inside the diner and was shown to a booth at the back of the restaurant and against the wall. He slid into the bench seat that faced the door. Perfect. She couldn't have chosen a better location herself. Had the hostess shown him to a booth any farther away, then Annie would've had a problem.

They'd arrived a half hour early with the intention of Luke taping the inexpensive recorder under the table close to where Joanne would sit. And then hope for the best. Annie was supposed to wait in the car under an oak tree at the far side of the parking lot.

Or so she'd told Luke.

The tinted-glass windows made it difficult to see

inside but, when she thought she saw him bend down to place the recorder, she got out and hurried toward the rear of the diner. A thirty-something dark-haired man, wearing a dirty apron and pulling a pack of cigarettes out of his pocket, stood near a door with an employees-only sign.

Annie pulled a folded twenty-dollar bill out of her pocket and kept it in her fist. She smiled as she approached the man.

He saw her, smiled back, and then gave her a quick once-over while he lit a cigarette. "The entrance is on the other side."

"I know, but I'm trying to surprise my boyfriend." She showed him the twenty. "I'd really like to go in through the back."

He plucked the bill out of her hand and then stepped away from the door. "Be my guest."

"Will anybody stop me?"

"Tell him Harold said it was okay." He stuffed the money in his pocket, took another drag and stared up at the puffy white clouds that had seemed to follow them from Hasting's Corner.

She opened the door and sneaked a peak inside before entering the kitchen. A fry cook looked up from the burger he was grilling and frowned at her. She told him what Harold said and, without a word, he went back to slapping cheese on the burger.

Another twenty from her pocket took care of a waitress who came through the swinging doors, and bought Annie a coke and a seat right to the back of

Luke. The brown-vinyl booth backs were high, which was a good thing because slumping a little made her invisible to the rest of the restaurant, but then she hoped it wouldn't be too hard to eavesdrop.

Ten minutes later, she found out.

With his back to her, Luke's voice was only slightly muffled when he said, "Hey, looking good, baby."

"Well, thank you, lover." Joanne actually giggled.

Oh, brother. Annie took a gulp of her coke. She knew Luke was buttering the woman up, but jeez. And Joanne? She had one of those annoying kind of southern drawls that only busty blondes seemed to have. Okay, that was stupid, but Annie was dying to know what Joanne looked like.

"Ah, no, why don't you sit on that side. That way I can look at you. Pretty dress, by the way."

"Thank you. You're early."

"So are you."

Joanne sighed. "Ernest isn't supposed to come home tonight, but you never know."

"He's away on business?"

"Amarillo. Even if he does come home, that gives us quite a bit of time."

At the silly tone of Joanne's voice, Annie gritted her teeth. Even though she couldn't see the woman, she could imagine the saucy come-hither smile. Women like that made her skin crawl.

"But he might, so how about we get down to business?"

"You're right." She lowered her voice to the point

Annie could barely hear her. "Remember the last time we came here?"

"Joanne, don't. I'm in a lot of trouble. I need your help or I won't be riding in Houston next month."

"My God, you can't be serious."

"What?"

"You can't ride anymore, sugar. You're finished, you know that. Every one of your doctors has written you off."

Luke noisily cleared his throat. "They don't know my body like I do. I can ride again."

The waitress interrupted to take Joanne's order, giving Annie a chance to catch her breath. Luke hadn't told her about what the doctors had said. Why not? She knew he was hurt but she had no idea the injury was supposed to have ended his career. She stared at the picture of a young Elvis on the wall where the blue wallpaper had started to fade.

If Luke couldn't ride anymore, he'd be hurting for money. Of course that didn't mean he'd steal it. Besides, if it were true, he wouldn't be so anxious to prove his innocence. Nor would he be so dumb as to stick around.

"Come on, baby." It was Joanne. "Don't be foolish. You can't afford to get hurt again." She hesitated. "Look," she said finally, her voice so low that Annie had to strain to hear. "I have some money put away. Enough to get us anywhere you want to go."

"What are you talking about?"

She laughed. "How does Rio sound? I've always wanted to go there."

"Damn it, Joanne, here I thought you wouldn't come forward because you were afraid of losing Seabrook. And his money."

"I thought I could do it. I did. But he's such a horrid man. I can barely stand to look at him anymore, much less have him touch me."

"Damn."

"Come on, Luke. We're good together. Admit it. You can heal, lying on a warm white sandy beach and not worrying about money."

Luke stayed silent so long, Annie tensed. Was he thinking about going with Joanne? No way. She'd merely taken him by surprise. He probably didn't know what to say.

The teenaged waitress in her fifties-style pink uniform stopped to see if Annie wanted another coke. She abruptly shook her head, not wanting Luke to hear her voice. Then the waitress asked if Annie wanted her check, causing her to miss part of Luke's response. She wasn't worried though, she'd hear it later on tape.

"Yeah, but I'd have to go back to work some time," Luke was saying.

"Not necessarily. Hey, let's go someplace where we can get a drink."

"I don't want a drink. I want to get Wilcox off my ass."

"Aren't you listening to me? We can be out of here by tomorrow. Just say the word."

"I'd rather you talk to Wilcox and clear me."

Joanne harrumphed. "Sorry, sugar, I can't do that."

"But you know I didn't steal the money."

"That's right, I do. And that's why I've offered you a way out. Leave with me tomorrow."

A long silence followed, and Annie wondered if Luke had come to the same conclusion she had.

"You're leaving with or without me, aren't you?" he asked and then, in obvious disbelief, added, "You stole the million dollars."

Joanne laughed. "Why would I have done that?"

"I should have known."

"There's a simple solution here. Come with me."

Luke hesitated. "A million dollars doesn't go that far these days."

"It would in South America." She made a throaty sound. "Assuming we had that much."

Come on, Luke. Annie's heart raced. If he could only get her to admit that she'd stolen the money. Even if they didn't get it on tape it would—

"I'd have to leave my Corvette..." Luke made it sound as if he were actually thinking about it. Good move. Better to catch her with the money on her.

"Luke, don't be such a mook. We'll get you another one."

Annie pressed her back against the brown vinyl, as if getting that fraction closer would allow her to hear them any better. Had she heard right? It sounded as if Joanne had used the term mook. A term unique to New York City. Even more specific, Brooklyn. So why would a southern belle like Joanne use that expression?

"Look Joanne, you better not be messing with me. I don't want to say okay, and then end up penniless and on a wanted list."

"Luke, baby, trust me. I can take care of both of us. Meet me at the Dallas-Fort Worth airport tomorrow morning at eleven-thirty, and I'll prove it to you."

"You better be on the level."

"Be there and you'll see. I promise you won't regret it, sugar."

"How will I find you?"

"Go to the Admiral's Club."

"The what?"

She laughed. "It's going to be so fun showing you the finer things in life. You get to the airport and ask a porter where it is. I'll be waiting."

Annie realized that the conversation was just about over and that they could get up at any moment. Quickly, she laid some money on the table and slid out of the booth. Without even a brief glance at Joanne, Annie headed toward the kitchen. Ignoring the employees' stares, she let herself out the back door and jogged to the car.

Five minutes after she got down low behind the wheel, Luke and Joanne walked out together, their arms linked. The woman was exactly as Annie had pictured her. A leggy blonde, wearing a ridiculously short, white leather skirt, and if her blouse were cut any lower, she would be arrested for indecency.

And then there was Luke. How could he still take Annie's breath away? How could she still think he was one of the best-looking men she'd ever seen? Tall and lean, muscles in all the right places and the clearest, bluest eyes, he was commercial material. Even the long, slow strides he took were sexier than hell. It wasn't fair.

She grudgingly watched him walk Joanne to a silver Mercedes convertible. He and Joanne talked for a couple of minutes, and then she wrapped her arms around him and shamelessly kissed him, open mouthed, oblivious to the passersby. He didn't seem to have a problem with the public display. In fact, he looked as if he were enjoying it, judging by the way he ran his hands down her back and then cupped her backside.

Just as he had done to Annie.

She bit her lower lip, not sure what it would accomplish. She wouldn't cry. Not over Luke. Not over anyone. Those days were over. Still, better that she didn't watch. She leaned her head back and stared at the beige felt that covered the roof.

If she didn't distance herself from Luke or the part he had to play, she wouldn't be of any help. And she needed to do this, if only for herself and for her career. How could she have been so foolish?

If any of this came to light, it would be over for her. It wouldn't matter if Luke was telling the truth. She'd become emotionally involved and helped him without any evidence as to his innocence. And she'd lied to the sheriff.

She brought her chin down and saw Luke heading

into the restaurant. Joanne was reversing the silver Mercedes out of the stall. Annie grabbed the door handle and then clued in to what he was doing. Going back for the recorder. Plastered against Joanne like he'd been, good thing he hadn't put it in his breast pocket.

As soon as Joanne's car disappeared, Luke walked out of the diner. He had something in his hand, presumably the recorder. She stayed slumped in the seat in case Joanne returned.

He must have feared the same thing because he went to the driver's side. She slid over as best she could without being seen. The tinted windows helped, but there was no sense taking any chances now.

He climbed behind the wheel and started the engine without looking at her. He kept his gaze on the street that Joanne had taken and then drove the car out onto the same street, but they headed in the opposite direction.

"How did it go?" she asked, shifting positions but not quite ready to sit upright yet.

"She did it. She took the money." He almost spat out the words.

"Are you sure?" Annie hoped she sounded surprised enough.

"She didn't come out and say it. But yeah, she took it, all right." The veins in his neck stuck out. His jaw was so tight he was liable to chip a tooth. "And she was gonna let me fry for it, the—" He shook his head.

"Don't start taking it personally."

"Yeah, right."

"That's when you screw up." She watched him, not sure which Luke to believe. The one who'd kissed Joanne like he wanted to strip her naked and get down and dirty right there in the middle of the parking lot, or this one, angry and hurt and scared, though he'd never admit it.

"So what did she want?"

Luke kept his eyes on the road. "She wants me to leave town."

Annie frowned. "That's it?"

"Basically."

She picked up the recorder.

He looked over at her. "Bad news. I don't think it worked."

He was lying. Annie's heart sank. He was lying. Now she knew exactly which Luke she was dealing with.

15

Luke stopped the car five miles outside of Hasting's Corner. "I think you'd better drive. I'll lie across the backseat again in case Wilcox is still around."

Annie dutifully got out and went around the front of the car. She could barely look at him as she slid in behind the wheel. The last hour and a half had been sheer torture. She wanted to rant at him, to tell him what a lowdown piece of scum he was, she wanted to slap him across the face so hard he'd end up in traction. Worst of all, the absolute worst, she wanted to cry.

Damn him. Twice he'd fooled her. Made a total ass out of her. So what that her career was in the toilet. She didn't deserve to wear the uniform. She had the instincts and good sense of a gnat. Then again, that was probably an insult to the poor insect.

"Hey, I'm sorry about the recording. I really am." Luke sounded so sincere that she wanted to hit him. "I don't know what happened. The first half is fine, and then everything went haywire. Maybe I bumped it with my knee."

She might have believed him if he'd come clean

about meeting Joanne at the airport tomorrow, but he'd lied. He claimed she wanted him to leave town, that she'd cover his expenses. He neglected to mention that Joanne would be accompanying him.

Half of her was tempted to deliver him directly to the sheriff. Take her chance that Wilcox would be grateful enough that he wouldn't say anything to her bosses in New York. But the other half of her wanted to play out the hand. Track Luke to the airport tomorrow and catch him and Joanne red-handed. She couldn't arrest him because she had no jurisdiction, but she could arrange something with the Dallas police.

"Now that I know Joanne stole the money, may-be I should go to Wilcox myself." Annie turned the wheel sharply. "I have his cell number. I could call him right now. Have him meet us at the house."

"No, I don't want you involved any further."

She smiled. Right. "I already told you, that ship has sailed."

"Not necessarily. Not now that we have proof it was Joanne."

"We have nothing."

"We know she has the money." Luke made a sound of disgust. "That may be enough. When we get to the house, I'll call Wilcox. He doesn't have to know where I'm calling from. In fact, I'll use my cell phone."

She dug in her pocket, found the sheriff's card and passed it over her shoulder. "Here. Call him now." At the awkward silence she smiled—wryly.

Finally he took the card and said, "I'll call him when we get back."

She didn't say anything else, mostly because she didn't trust herself to speak. She couldn't let on that she knew what he was up to. Why ruin the surprise?

"Annie?"

"Yeah."

"We had something good going," he said, and she nearly hit the brakes to physically kick him out of the car. "I hope someday you can forgive me."

"Don't count on it," she murmured, not caring if he heard her or not. She would never, ever be so gullible again.

JOANNE THREW her car keys on the console table in the foyer. She stopped to pluck a pink rose out of the bouquet of fresh cut flowers sitting in the large crystal vase. Twice a week, three fresh bouquets were delivered for Yolanda to place in the bedroom, the formal living room and the foyer. Joanne sighed. She'd miss this small amenity, and her new Mercedes. God, that car was the best one she'd managed to get her hands on yet. But Seabrook was also the biggest pig she'd had to put up with.

Just thinking about the sweaty pompous slob made her shudder. If she played her cards right, this morning was the last time she'd ever see his saggy jowls. Or smell his rank cigar breath again. The thought cheered her as she headed for his study.

First, she'd look for all his hiding places where she

knew he stashed ill-gotten cash. She was aware of two of them, but she suspected there were others. The vault under his desk, she'd already cleaned out. Ernest had kept the million in prize money there, the total contribution made by his fellow stockmen, along with another fifty thousand of his own money. Hers now.

She smiled. She had to call the airlines and check on tomorrow's flight to New York. If she could've, she would have left tonight, but too many loose ends needed tying up. Not the least of which was digging up the money she'd buried near the bathhouse.

His study doors were closed, as usual, but hopefully they weren't locked. She'd barely put her hand on the doorknob when Yolanda appeared almost from nowhere. The bitch had probably been spying on her.

The maid stood not four feet away, her hands folded, her eyebrows arched slightly. "May I help you, señora?"

"Does it look like I need help?"

Yolanda gave her a predictably patronizing smile. Something else Joanne wouldn't miss. "Señor Seabrook does not wish to be disturbed."

Panic filled her lungs so that she couldn't breathe. "He's here?"

The bitch had the audacity to smile. "No, señora, I meant he does not like his things disturbed."

"I don't think he meant me." Joanne smiled back. "But thank you for being so attentive."

Yolanda lost the smile. She stood uncertainly, resentment simmering in her dark eyes.

"You can go now." Joanne gestured dismissively, pleased to catch the anger in Yolanda's face before the maid turned and retraced her steps down the hall.

Joanne waited a few moments to be sure the bitch didn't sneak back, and then slipped through the double mahogany doors. She'd always hated the heavy darkness of the room, from the black walnut paneling to the dingy brown Oriental rugs that cost a fortune but looked like crap. Because Seabrook had no taste. None whatsoever. The fat uncouth slob.

But he was rich. And stupid—when it came to her, anyway. She'd made sure of that. After all, it was her job.

She checked the credenza first, cursing when she broke one of her red acrylic nails. Nothing in the drawers. She turned to the desk just as the phone rang. She grabbed it before Yolanda could answer.

"Joanne? I'm surprised you're home." It was Ernest.

She swiveled his chair around and sank into it. Just hearing his voice disgusted her. "Where else would I be?"

He chuckled. "Come now. I'm not totally blind."

She pressed her lips together to keep from saying something snide. Thank God tomorrow it would all be over. "So, I trust everything is going well?"

"Fine," he muttered. "Has Wilcox called?"

"As a matter of fact he did. This morning."

"He find McCall yet?"

She hesitated. If she said no and he found out otherwise, he could get suspicious and come home early. "Haven't you called him? He's expecting you to."

"The son of a bitch isn't answering his damn phone."

Joanne frowned. What was that about? Maybe he'd taken her bait and was on his way here. That would change everything. She didn't need him now. In fact, he could be a liability.

"Joanne?" He puffed on his cigar. "Woman, are you there?"

"Yes, Ernest, I'm here." She had to think fast. If she called Jethro, would he pick up? She could tell him Ernest had come home tonight, after all. But first she had to get rid of Ernest. "Have I told you how much I miss you, baby?" she asked in that sexy adoring tone he loved her to use. "So why don't you go hurry and finish that business of yours so you can come home to me?"

"Well, darlin', that's one of the reasons I was calling. Looks like I might make it home tonight, after all."

Joanne dropped the phone on her lap. "Oh, shit."

LUKE STRETCHED OUT on the bed in the guest room, his hands clasped behind his head and stared at the ceiling. He shouldn't be lying here alone while Annie was by herself in the other room. It just didn't seem right. They'd been so good together. He couldn't remember ever being so comfortable with a woman. He'd told her things about himself, things he'd normally rather die than admit to anyone. And she'd understood.

He felt like a heel having to lie to her. It was for her own good, but he was pretty sure she wouldn't see it that way if she discovered his plan. He knew she was angry about the recorder. Good thing she didn't know that he'd purposely messed it up to protect her. She thought that a taped confession would be enough, but she didn't understand how things worked around here. The rich had all the power. They were the law. The only sure way this could end well was to catch Joanne with the money.

Otherwise, it wouldn't surprise him one bit if Seabrook tried to save face by still pinning the theft on Luke. Better than have everyone know what a fool he'd been to be conned by Joanne. To a guy like Seabrook, Luke was disposable, a nobody. Who would care if he spent the rest of his life in prison?

Luke swallowed hard. Sadly, the truth was that no one would care. Annie may have, if things had gone differently. But he'd screwed that up, too. Just like he'd messed up most everything else in his life. The only thing he'd ever done well was ride horses and bulls, and now that was over.

He hated to face that sorry truth, but that wouldn't make it go away. For the past few days he was finally starting to get it. He'd been hurt many times before and mended quickly. Not this time. His shoulder had suffered one too many tears, and he wasn't twenty-five anymore.

If by some fluke he got out of this trouble, he still wanted to try his hand at ranching, and that required physical labor. He'd be no good to anyone, least of all himself. As if there'd be anyone, anyway. His fault. Annie was right: he pushed women away.

There'd been one woman, five years ago, he could've been happy with. Sweet and pretty, Greta was a schoolteacher in Oklahoma City and she didn't give a rat's ass that he'd consistently won first place in every major rodeo from here to Wyoming. She said she liked him because he was kind and a real gentleman. She didn't know him at all. Didn't matter. The afternoon he was supposed to meet her parents, he'd gotten drunk instead, and never called Greta again. What a cruel ass he'd been. Thank God he'd grown up.

He closed his eyes, and there was Annie's face. The wide golden-hazel eyes, her long untamed hair, the tiny beauty mark on her left cheekbone. He could tell she'd had freckles once, but they'd mostly faded, only a few remained across the bridge of her nose that disappeared each morning after she applied makeup. Even that she wore little of, which he liked a lot.

Hell, there wasn't anything he didn't like about her. And as with everything else in his life, he screwed up any possibility for them, too. Yep, Annie was better off without him, anyway.

He couldn't put it off any longer. He sat up and then planted his boots on the floor. On the nightstand was his cell phone and the card with Wilcox's number. Luke picked them both up.

If his plan went south, Wilcox would be deeper in Seabrook's pocket than Luke knew. But at least

Annie wouldn't be involved. No one ever needed to know he even knew her. If she wanted, she could pretend they'd never met. The thought was more painful than being stomped on by a mad bull.

He swallowed hard again and then flipped his phone open, startled when it rang at the same time, especially since his service was spotty out here. He checked the caller's number on the screen. It was Joanne. Now what?

ANNIE PACED to the window and glanced at the bedside clock. Nine-ten. Which meant it was eleven-ten New York time. Why hadn't Lisa called back by now? If she hadn't found anything on Joanne, the woman had no priors, or it could mean she was an opportunist who'd never been caught or kept her crimes small enough that she stayed under the radar.

Which wouldn't be bad. In this instance it would be much easier dealing with an amateur, although Annie wanted to know who she was up against. She didn't even know if she could trust Wilcox. All she had was Luke's word that Wilcox might be Seabrook's puppet. But with Luke it was hard to tell what were lies and what were truths.

The reminder physically hurt. Her stomach had knotted some time on the ride back and hadn't let up in spite of all the antacid tabs she'd popped. Once she heard from Lisa, she'd feel better. Then she could contact the Dallas police, tell them what she knew and have a detective meet her at the airport. To arrest Joanne. And Luke.

Oh, God. How could this be happening? How could she have been so wrong about Luke? She'd have to leave this bedroom some time, and that was going to be hard. Knowing but having to pretend that she didn't know he had betrayed her.

Chester was another problem. She had to keep him in the dark. It was going to break his heart about Luke, and she couldn't ignore the possibility that he'd warn Luke. She didn't think so, but still. Anyway, why should she have to be the one to tell him?

She'd talked to Aunt Marjorie an hour ago and found out she'd be released from the hospital tomorrow. Thankfully it would all be over by then. Aunt Marjorie certainly didn't need the excitement. As far as the repairs around the ranch, Annie would have a lot of time to help out.

First, the department would put her on leave to investigate her involvement, and then... Oh, man, she so didn't want to see her captain's face when he found out how naive she'd been. And even that wouldn't be as bad as being compared to her father. Nothing could be worse. Yup, she'd really done it this time.

The phone rang, and she grabbed it in the middle of the first ring.

"You ready for this?" Lisa blurted, with excitement.

"Go."

"We don't have a match on the name but, from your description, I think I've found her. Real name is

Melinda Sweeney, age thirty-four, prefers to pass herself off as late twenties. Naturally blond but sometimes goes auburn. Green eyes, about five-six and can do a number of accents. Is all this sounding like her?"

"I think so. Is she from New York?"

"Born and bred in Brooklyn. She still has family here. But she's spent some time in Florida and the south."

Annie exhaled slowly. Sure sounded like the right woman. "So why do we have a sheet on her?"

Lisa snorted. "Her last two husbands disappeared. One during a boating trip, after two years of marriage, and the other on a safari in Africa, again after two years. Oh, did I tell you? She likes her guys filthy rich."

"And then dead," Annie murmured. Was that Luke's fate if he ran off with this woman? He didn't have money, but maybe she had enough so now all she wanted was a partner. Mindless sex—until maybe she got tired of him, too.

"So it would seem. Unfortunately, no one's been able to pin anything on her. No bodies, lots of ocean, foreign countries, and all that. Tough to make a case."

"Yeah." Annie was going to fix that. She couldn't nail Joanne for murder, but grand larceny would earn Mrs. Seabrook a nice, lengthy prison sentence. In the meantime, maybe Annie could dig up more evidence regarding the alleged murders.

"There is one other thing, though, that's kind of interesting. She was first married right out of high school to some college kid. After only a year, he died from a fall while the two of them were hiking. Six months later she married her second husband."

"Did they suspect foul play with the first one?"

"They had no reason to."

"But we do now." Annie smiled. She was going to sift through the records on that accident like there was no tomorrow.

"Okay, I've gotten you everything you asked for, on my night off, I might add, not that I minded. I was happy to do it even without an explanation from you. But, girl, I'm dying to know what's happening."

Annie sighed. "Look, it's a long story. I promise I'll fill you in on everything tomorrow, but right now I have to go."

It took Lisa a moment before she asked, "Are you in some kind of trouble?"

"No." Annie lied to her best friend for the first time.

"Okay," she said slowly, uncertainly.

"Thanks, Lisa. You're the best." Annie hung up before she did something silly, like blubbering.

She went to the mirror and checked to make sure the skin below her eyes wasn't smudged, and then ran a quick brush through her hair. It wasn't going to be easy acting as if everything was all right, but she had to do it. With any luck, Luke had already gone to bed, but she doubted it.

He'd been edgy and preoccupied from the time they got home until she excused herself, claiming she needed a nap. Neither one of them had felt like dinner. Unfortunately, Chester ate by himself in the bunkhouse, as he often did. Tonight a buffer would've been nice.

She opened the bedroom door and saw that the hall was dark. In fact, there were no lights on in the entire house. A bad feeling gnawed at her, and she quietly made her way to Luke's room. She turned the knob ever so slowly and opened the door a crack. He was lying in bed, and it was really him, not pillows propped under the sheets. He was lying on his back on top of the covers, wearing only boxers.

Mostly it was his silhouette that was visible only because of the full moon shining in through the open window. But it was easy to fill in the blanks. She had every inch of him memorized. The powerful thigh muscles from riding for so many years, the perfectly flat stomach with its ridges of muscle that she loved running her palms over.

She closed her eyes. This had to stop. That was another time, another Luke. She looked at him again, this time to be sure he hadn't stirred, and then she moved to leave.

"Don't go."

His gruff whisper stilled her feet and her heart. She should pretend she hadn't heard him, shut the door and walk away.

"I didn't go to my grandfather's funeral," he said, "because I was ashamed. Not of him. Of myself. I tried to say it was because the old man never stood up for me when my mother went off, but that was only part of the story."

Annie didn't dare turn to face him, although she couldn't force herself to leave.

"I may not have been a lot of things my mother called me, but the woman knew I was selfish. Hell, maybe I became selfish after hearing it all my life. It doesn't matter why. It's just the truth. When I ran into you, all I thought about was how I could use you. How I could hide here so that I could clear my name. I didn't for a minute consider that it might get you involved in something bad. That there were consequences for you. I moved in, took advantage of your kindness."

With a heavy heart, she continued to stare at the door. So she was right about everything. He'd admitted his role, and she should hate him for it. He was a selfish bastard, everything she should have been wary of. And yet, she'd slept in his arms. She'd made love to him. And, God help her, the pull to do it again was still there.

"I just want you to know that I'm sorry," he said, his voice cracking on the last word. "You deserve so much better. You deserve a man I couldn't hope to be. I am the man my mother said I was. But now…"

She swallowed, was determined not to let the trembling she felt inside show through. "Now?"

"I want to be the man you thought I was."

"Good night, Luke," she said. But what she really meant was goodbye.

16

THE DREAM was so real Annie bolted upright, her heart beat so hard it reverberated in her ears. But she was still in her aunt's room, and there'd been no gunshots. She looked at the alarm clock. Only a little after five.

She lay down, knowing there was no way she'd go back to sleep, although she hadn't expected to fall asleep in the first place. She closed her eyes and replayed scenes from yesterday. Luke had seemed so earnest about clearing his name. Whether he'd admit it or not, he wanted to prove his mother wrong. To show the entire town that he wasn't the loser she'd painted him to be. So what had happened? Had he simply given up?

Something creaked, it sounded like a floorboard. She opened her eyes and stared at the bedroom door. Slowly it opened. She caught a glimpse of Luke, and then she closed her eyes again. Yes, she truly was insane. A normal person would have been afraid. She wasn't. Only curious. Was he making sure she was asleep so he could take off?

She lay perfectly still, her lashes lifted only a sliver so she could watch him enter and approach her bed. He stood there watching her for so long that her curiosity was replaced with fear so thick it clogged her throat. She fisted her hands beneath the covers, ready to defend herself.

All he did was gently push the hair away from her face, then bent down and kissed her forehead. "I'm sorry, darlin'," he whispered so softly that she wasn't sure she'd heard correctly. "I'll miss you."

He lightly kissed her lips, then he pulled back and watched her. Agonizingly, she continued to pretend she was asleep, even though her frustration threatened to explode. He'd miss her? The bastard couldn't even be honest with himself.

Only after she heard him at the door did she open her eyes more. He was fully dressed, including his boots. The guy was going to run.

Good luck, Luke McCall. He wasn't about to escape on her watch.

LUKE CLIMBED in the truck and started the old engine. Damn good thing he was parked in the barn or the racket would've woken everyone up. As it was, Chester probably heard him since the bunkhouse was directly behind the barn. He'd wonder where Luke was going, but he wouldn't think that much of it.

If Annie heard, on the other hand, she'd come running out with a shotgun. Not that he'd blame her. He simply had no choice. Not only had Joanne moved up the time to meet, but Luke couldn't very well let Annie tag along.

He backed out of the barn, stopped, got out and closed the door, all the while praying that the engine wouldn't die, because he couldn't gun it like he usually had to. Once back behind the wheel, he crawled to the driveway hoping the sheriff had given up his vigil by now. Luke patted the dashboard, coaxing the truck to keep plugging away until he got to the road. Once he was on blacktop, he gunned the engine and sped as fast as he could toward the Dallas-Fort Worth airport.

JOANNE GLANCED over her shoulder, half expecting to see that rancid slob Earnest, sweating like one of his hogs, running down the terminal corridor toward her. He had to know something was up. Why else would he have lied about returning from Amarillo last night and not shown up? Oh, hell, she was being paranoid. He probably only meant to keep her in check. Ruin any party plans she might have had in his absence.

Still, she wasn't taking any chances. After Yolanda and Margarita had left for the evening, she'd dug up the money and packed it with the clothes she couldn't bear to leave behind and then loaded her Mercedes and headed for the airport Marriott.

A bump in the carpet knocked her rolling bag askew and she struggled to keep it upright. A million-plus bucks in cash wasn't easy to maneuver. She hated doing business this way. Life insurance policies and straight community property settlements were far cleaner but, if she'd had to put up with that pig for another day, she couldn't trust herself to not put a bullet in his fat head. That would've been difficult to explain.

She saw a sign about twenty yards away for the Admiral's Club but no sign of Luke. She checked her watch. It was early, but she'd expected him to be here by now, waiting outside, since he wasn't a member. But knowing Luke, if there was a woman at the reception desk, screw the membership requirement, he'd have the red carpet laid out for him.

There sure was something about the man that made her juices flow. He'd been a totally unexpected pleasure when she'd met him at the rodeo five months ago. This had been the first time she'd had an affair while married to one of her marks. Big mistake— every minute she spent with Luke had made living with Seabrook that much more unbearable.

The availability of the million in cash had been a stroke of luck, so she'd decided to cut her losses even though Seabrook was worth fifty times that much. Luke had been another loss she'd been willing to bear...at first. In the end, she wasn't able to resist taking that fine body with her. She sure as hell hoped it wasn't a mistake.

She checked her watch again, getting worried this time. The airport was horribly crowded, which meant even she'd be delayed. He'd come. If not for her, for the money. She looked around again and then she saw him, coming from the direction of the elevators. He stood out from the crowd, tall, lean in dark blue jeans, that sexy black Stetson hat on his head. She smiled as he got closer.

"I'm not late, am I?" he asked.

She tilted her head back for a kiss. He seemed reluctant to at first, and then he annoyingly brushed her lips with his. Hardly a kiss at all. Maybe he was nervous. He'd relax once they got on the plane.

"Nope. You're fine. If seats on an earlier flight become available, I want to grab them. By the way, Ernest didn't come home last night. The stupid prick had the nerve to check up on me."

Luke was frowning at her. "What happened to your accent?"

She laughed. "I'd heard Ernest liked his women southern and docile. I'm actually from New York. Ready?"

"Sure."

"You don't have a bag?"

"It would've looked suspicious. Had to just bring myself."

She nodded and turned toward the club's door. "Right. Good thinking. Don't you worry, we'll go shopping and you can buy anything you want."

"Here, let me help you with that."

She shook her head. "No, thanks. I'm not letting this bag out of my sight—or my clutches."

Luke stared at it in awe. In a voice only she could hear, he asked, "You fit all that money in there?"

Joanne smiled. "And then some."

Luke smiled back. They had her now. No sweet talking her way out of this one. He looked over his shoulder and found Wilcox right where he was supposed to be, hiding behind a newspaper. The sheriff caught his signal and got to his feet.

Joanne's horrified gaze fixed on Wilcox. "What the hell?" She started slowly backing up.

"Luke, stop right there." It was Annie's voice. "Both of you."

He glanced around but couldn't see her. And then he did, coming out of a crowd of Japanese tourists, she had her badge in her hand, facing out to him. Her other hand was hidden in the blue blazer she wore, probably resting on the gun he'd turned over to her.

"Don't make this more difficult than it has to be," she said as she got closer.

Joanne let go of the bag and turned to run. A heavyset man in a nylon windbreaker caught her by the arm. She tried to twist away and, in the scuffle, Luke saw the badge clipped to his belt.

Looking confused, Annie frowned at the man, and then she looked at Luke again.

Sheriff Wilcox joined them. He stooped down and picked up the handle on the bag of money. The cop in the windbreaker was cuffing Joanne and reading her rights, while she struggled and yelled a string of obscenities at him and Wilcox.

Wilcox just smiled at her and, when she'd run out of gas, he said, "You know, Mrs. Seabrook, they search luggage nowadays. Even rich people's luggage. There's no way in heaven or hell you'd have put one foot on that plane."

She cursed him again. Him and all his progeny.

Annie stood there speechless. She turned to stare at Luke, the look in her eyes making him want to turn back time. He reached out to take her hand but she wouldn't let him. "Come on, Annie. Let me explain."

"You made me look like a fool."

"No, I was trying to protect you."

Her disbelieving laugh sounded as if it might turn into a sob. "You've been working with the sheriff all along. What, did you think I was some dumb cop from New York?"

"No. No." He took her by the arm, becoming gently insistent when she tried to pull away. Interested onlookers gathered around them so he steered her toward a private spot. "I called him last night and filled him in on my meeting with Joanne so we could catch her with the money."

"But you lied to me. Why? I told you I'd help."

He glanced over at Wilcox who seemed far too interested in Annie and him. Luke hadn't said anything about her to the sheriff. This is exactly what Luke was afraid of. Now Annie was involved, and he had no idea how he was going to convince Wilcox that she was the innocent in all this.

"Let's talk about this later, okay?" He urged her toward the elevator, plowing a path through the stubborn crowd. "I'll probably have to go with the sheriff and give a statement or something, but then I'll meet you at your aunt's ranch. I promise."

Annie stared at him. She should be ecstatic that he'd never planned on running off with Joanne. But she wasn't. Why couldn't he have trusted her to help him? "Why should I believe anything you say?"

"Annie, please, leave now. We'll talk later. Please, Annie." He looked so sincere, but she'd seen that look—a second before he'd lied his ass off.

"Well, now, isn't this interesting?" Sheriff Wilcox had followed them, Joanne's rolling bag firmly in his grasp. "Sergeant Corrigan, I could swear you told me you never met Luke McCall."

She stared at the sheriff. "Yes, um, well…" Now she knew why Luke had tried to get rid of her. "To tell you the truth, I wasn't sure you weren't in on framing Luke."

"Really?" Wilcox chuckled. "And how did you know he'd been framed?"

Heat stung her cheeks. What could she say? Admit that she'd foolishly allowed herself to be used? That Luke had told her he was innocent and that she'd believed him, without any evidence? She didn't deserve to keep her badge.

"I got another question." Wilcox narrowed his gaze. "Were you prepared to arrest Luke and Joanne by yourself? You didn't come with backup."

Her gaze met Luke's. He seemed anxious for her answer. Damn him. Even with everything she knew, she'd hoped he wouldn't go through with hightailing it with Joanne.

She sighed. "Look, Sheriff, you're right. Let's go to your—"

Luke stepped in front of her and faced Wilcox. "I was there when you came to the ranch. In the room, listening to what she told you. I had a gun. I told her I'd shoot both of you if she gave me up."

Annie tried to push him out of her way. "That's a lie."

The sheriff looked from Luke to Annie. "You were holding her hostage in that house?"

"Yes, sir, I was."

"You're definitely going to need a lawyer, son."

"Luke, don't be an idiot," she insisted. "Do you have any idea what you're saying? I know you're just trying to protect me." As soon as she said the words, she knew it was true. He'd made a mistake in the beginning by not being honest but, after that, he hadn't used her or her badge, he'd tried to protect her. "Luke, you're confessing to kidnapping. You'll go to prison for a very long time."

He looked scared, she could tell. "I know, but it's the truth."

"Don't do this," she said softly, hoping the sheriff couldn't hear her. "You want everyone in Hasting's Corner to think your mom was right about you?"

Anger flashed across his face. He put his hands out, wrists together. "Come on, Sheriff, let's go."

"This is your life we're talking about, Luke, and you're worried about my stinking career." Annie pulled the badge from her pocket and held it out to

Wilcox. "Here. Take it. Not him. He's lying. I was a willing party."

"No." Luke pushed her hand with the badge away from the sheriff.

"All right, that's enough you two." Wilcox rubbed his jaw and sighed heavily, looking at Annie he said, "You had a duty as a law officer to turn this boy in. You know that, I know that. We all make mistakes. It turned out well. I don't see any need for stirring up more trouble."

"You mean—"

He ignored her and looked at Luke. "You better stay away from married women."

"No kidding." Luke slid a sheepish glance at Annie.

"I will have to take a statement, since the Dallas police are involved now. Detective Rodriguez has kindly escorted Mrs. Seabrook to his station."

"Don't let them get the collar, Sheriff. Mrs. Seabrook has got one hell of a history."

Both men looked questioningly at her. She gave them a brief rundown of the information Lisa had provided. She stayed calm and was articulate, when all she wanted to do was jump and scream and hug Luke until he couldn't breathe. Until the tears she was holding back burst from her in a downpour.

The sacrifice Luke had been willing to make to maintain her innocence was more than she could comprehend. She felt alive with emotions she hadn't known existed. Fearful she'd fall apart at any moment, she quickly wrapped it up with a promise to have Lisa fax the information to the sheriff's office.

"Thanks, Sergeant," Wilcox told her. "I'm headed to the station now. Afraid you'll have to come, too, McCall."

"No problem." Luke tentatively smiled at Annie. "Am I welcome back at the ranch when I'm done?"

"You don't show up and I'll hunt you down."

He really smiled then and swooped in for a brief kiss. "I'll hurry."

WATCHING THEM, Wilcox grinned and shook his head. Maybe there was hope for him yet. Maybe love wasn't just a tall tale told by old Texans. Then again, he couldn't afford any more alimony.

17

As soon as Annie got to the ranch she called Lisa and arranged for Sheriff Wilcox to receive the information about Joanne Seabrook. Next, she filled Chester in on what had happened. In typical Chester fashion, he just nodded and said he knew Luke was no criminal. Fortunately for Chester, he went back to his chores, otherwise, Annie would have had to politely throw him out so she could get ready before Luke returned.

This time, there wasn't a doubt in her mind that he would come back. The shock over what he'd done hadn't worn off yet. He'd been willing to go to prison, rather than involve her. Mind-boggling. Every time she thought about it, she got goose bumps.

After what seemed like an eon, she heard the truck coming down the drive. She ran to the window, but it wasn't his truck after all, but a red Corvette. Part of the conversation in the diner came back to her, and she knew it was Luke behind the wheel. Sure enough, he parked close to the house and ran up the steps.

He burst through the door, relief on his face when he saw her. Without a word he wrapped his arms around her and lifted her off the floor, kissing her lips, her cheek, her neck.

She laughed. "Hey, slow down."

"When I left here this morning, I didn't know if I'd ever see you again."

She touched his face and he set her back on the floor. "Thank you."

"For what? Making your life miserable for the past few weeks?"

"You know what I mean."

"Hey, I've got a proposition for you. How about we do all the talking later."

"Great idea, McCall. Best idea I've heard in a long time."

He pulled her toward the bedroom. "Still talking."

She opened her mouth to give him the business, but then she just smiled, and let him take her away.

The second he closed the bedroom door, he had her shirt half unbuttoned, and she'd had his belt undone. Annie was in a panic, certain if she didn't get him naked and in bed in the next ten seconds, she'd burst into tears.

Luke seemed as crazed, and damn if they didn't make it to the bed before even one tear fell.

He pulled her tight against him as he kissed her senseless. Everything else fell away except the man and how he touched her. How he felt under her exploring hands. It was as if she'd never been with him before, that he was totally new. Or maybe she wasn't plain old Annie Corrigan anymore.

"I can't believe I almost lost you," he said, his lips inches from her own. "I wouldn't have cared if I had to go to prison. It wouldn't have made any difference."

She almost dismissed the words as cowboy charm, but then it hit her that Luke had nothing to gain by fancy talk. She was his, and he knew it. Only... "Aunt Marjorie is coming home."

He looked crestfallen. "When?"

"Tonight."

His hands stopped moving then. "Don't go, Annie."

"I have to. I'm her ride."

He slapped her butt, but she didn't get mad. She'd like to do some slapping of her own. "That's not what I meant."

Her eyes closed and she buried her face in his neck. He smelled so good. "I have no choice."

"Yes you do."

She looked up again. "Luke—"

"Wilcox told me he thought you had good instincts. And that there was going to be an opening for a new sheriff in about three months."

"Come on, Luke. You know—"

"Hey," he said, staring right into her eyes. "I'm telling you what the man said."

"He thought I had good instincts?"

Luke nodded. "He also said you wouldn't have any problem getting elected, being Luke McCall's woman and all."

It was her turn to slap his butt. "He did not say that."

"You're right, darlin', he didn't. But we both know it's the stone-cold truth."

"That I could get elected, or that I'm Luke McCall's woman?"

Luke leaned down and kissed her until she couldn't see straight. Then he lifted his lips and said, "Both, Annie. Both."

Epilogue

Four months later

RED, WHITE AND BLUE streamers were looped around the rafters and suspended from the ceiling. Brownies, cakes and cookies courtesy of Chester and Luke were put out in the barn for the occasion. Pictures of Annie, so big they showed every flaw on her face, covered the walls. The barn was barely recognizable.

Annie glanced around at all the people who'd come to her pre-victory party, insisted upon and organized by Aunt Marjorie, who'd recently received a clean bill of health. Annie hadn't wanted the fanfare. She knew her winning was a long shot—she was the new kid on the block. People didn't usually vote for newcomers although, bless him, Jethro had upped her chance.

Before he'd left for California, Jethro had leaked a lot about how Seabrook had tried to manipulate the local law enforcers. People weren't happy about Jethro's decision not to run again nor about what he'd said concerning Seabrook, and some stinging editorials in the local paper had resulted.

She smiled at Luke who was speaking with Aunt Marjorie. He'd been everything to Annie in the past four months. Friend, lover and even campaign manager. That had been a real treat. He'd never truly gotten the hang of diplomacy.

But he'd been there for her, even when she wasn't sure she could leave New York and had gone back for a month. After a week, she'd given notice to her captain. Her mind wasn't on the job anymore. She worried about whether Aunt Marjorie was sneaking sweets and if Chester was trying to do too much outside. Luke kept an eye on them, while he worked on the ranch his granddad had left him, and he visited her in New York on weekends. But it wasn't enough. Not even close.

"Nervous?" Even Lisa had come for the big announcement.

"A little. If I don't win, Aunt Marjorie and Luke are going to be so disappointed."

Lisa's brows went up. "And you won't be?"

Annie grinned. "So, have you found a good-looking cowboy yet?"

"Two. I can't believe there's actually a choice out here. Think you'll need a deputy?"

Annie laughed. "Let's see if I win first."

Lisa leaned over, her eyes shining with tears, and whispered, "You've already won."

"Don't you dare do that," Annie ordered. If she started crying, she'd shoot Lisa.

"Hey, what's going on?" Luke was suddenly beside her, putting an arm around her shoulders. "You okay?"

She nodded and blinked a couple of times.

"Excuse me." Lisa wiped at her eyes and smiled. "I think I see Mr. Right."

Luke barely waited for her to walk away. He turned to face Annie and brought her chin up to look deep into her eyes. "You miss New York and Lisa, don't you?"

"No, I mean, yes, I miss Lisa and her family. But did I make the right decision? You bet."

"What about school? You miss it?" He looked so worried.

"School was a substitute. What else did I have to do at night without you?"

Smiling, he slid his arms around her waist. "I never thought I could miss someone as much as I missed you."

She looped her arms about his neck. "Let's hope that never happens again."

"Nope. Got to stick around and take care of the folks there." Luke inclined his head toward Aunt Marjorie and Chester, who seemed to be engaged in their favorite pastime, bickering over something or other. It was probably over her new healthy eating regimen, which she'd thrust on Chester.

A sudden lump lodged in Annie's throat. They were a family, a real honest-to-goodness family. She opened her mouth to share her realization, but Luke nodded and said, "I know. Great isn't it?"

"Hey, everyone." It was Billy, red-faced and panting. He stopped running and was searching the crowd for his quarry before he broke the news. "Congratu-lations, Sheriff Corrigan!"

Cheers erupted. Luke picked her up and twirled her around, saying something she couldn't possibly hear over the racket. He set her down and camera flashes went off.

Damn it. In tomorrow's paper, there'd be a picture of the new sheriff crying like a girl.

* * * * *

Turn the page for a sneak preview of
IF I'D NEVER KNOWN YOUR LOVE
by
Georgia Bockoven

From the brand-new series
Harlequin Everlasting Love
Every great love has a story to tell. ™

One year, five months and four days missing

There's no way for you to know this, Evan, but I haven't written to you for a few months. Actually, it's been almost a year. I had a hard time picking up a pen once more after we paid the second ransom and then received a letter saying it wasn't enough. I was so sure you were coming home that I took the kids along to Bogotá so they could fly home with you and me, something I swore I'd never do. I've fallen in love with Colombia and the people who've opened their hearts to me. But fear is a constant companion when I'm there. I won't ever expose our children to that kind of danger again.

I'm at a loss over what to do anymore, Evan. I've begged and pleaded and thrown temper tantrums with every official I can corner both here and at home. They've been incredibly tolerant and understanding, but in the end as in-effectual as the rest of us.

I try to imagine what your life is like now, what you do every day, what you're wearing, what you eat. I want to believe that the people who have you are misguided yet kind, that they treat you well. It's how I survive day to day. To think of you being mistreated hurts too much. If I picture you locked away some-where and suffering, a weight descends on me that makes it almost impossible to get out of bed in the morning.

Your captors surely know you by now. They have to recognize what a good man you are. I imagine you working with their children, telling them that you have children, too, show-ing them the pictures you carry in your wallet. Can't the men who have you understand how much your children miss you? How can it not matter to them?

How can they keep you away from us all this time? Over and over, we've done what they asked. Are they oblivious to the depth of their cruelty? What kind of people are they that they don't care?

I used to keep a calendar beside our bed next to the peach rose you picked for me before you left. Every night I marked another day, counting how many you'd been gone. I don't do that any longer. I don't want to be reminded of all the days we'll never get back.

When I can't sleep at night, I tell you about my day. I imagine you hearing me and smiling over the details that make up my life now. I never tell you how defeated I feel at moments or how hard I work to hide it from everyone for fear they will see it as a reason to stop believing you are coming home to us.

And I couldn't tell you about the lump I found in my breast and how difficult it was going through all the tests without you here to lean on. The lump was benign—the process reaching that diagnosis utterly terrifying. I couldn't stop thinking about what would happen to Shelly and Jason if something happened to me.

We need you to come home.

I'm worn down with missing you.

I'm going to read this tomorrow and will probably tear it up or burn it in the fireplace. I don't want you to get the idea I ever doubted what I was doing to free you or thought the work a burden. I would gladly spend the rest of my life at it, even if, in the end, we only had one day together.

You are my life, Evan.

I will love you forever.

* * * * *

Don't miss this deeply moving
Harlequin Everlasting Love story about
a woman's struggle to bring back her kidnapped
husband from Colombia and her turmoil over
whether to let go, finally, and welcome another
man into her life.
IF I'D NEVER KNOWN YOUR LOVE
by Georgia Bockoven
is available March 27, 2007.

And also look for
THE NIGHT WE MET
by Tara Taylor Quinn,
a story about finding love
when you least expect it.

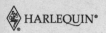

HARLEQUIN® *Romance*®

presents a brand-new trilogy by

PATRICIA THAYER

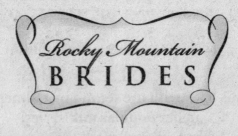

Rocky Mountain BRIDES

Three sisters come home to wed.

In April don't miss
Raising the Rancher's Family,

followed by
The Sheriff's Pregnant Wife,
on sale May 2007,

and

A Mother for the Tycoon's Child,
on sale June 2007.

REQUEST YOUR FREE BOOKS!

2 FREE NOVELS PLUS 2 FREE GIFTS!

HARLEQUIN®

Blaze®

Red-hot reads!

Silhouette® Desire

Introducing talented new author

TESSA RADLEY

*making her Silhouette Desire debut
this April with*

BLACK WIDOW BRIDE

Book #1794
Available in April 2007.

Wealthy Damon Asteriades had no choice but to
force Rebecca Grainger back to his family's estate—
despite his vow to keep away from her seductive
charms. But being so close to the woman society once
dubbed the Black Widow Bride had him aching to
claim her as his own...at any cost.

On sale April from Silhouette Desire!

Available wherever books are sold,
including most bookstores, supermarkets,
discount stores and drugstores.

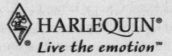

HARLEQUIN®

Blaze™

COMING NEXT MONTH

#315 COMING UNDONE Stephanie Tyler

There's a bad boy in camouflage knocking at Carly Winters's door, and she knows she's in trouble. The erotic fax that Jonathon "Hunt" Huntington's waving in her face—she can explain; how the buff Navy SEAL got ahold of it—she can't. But she sure wants to find out!

#316 SEX AS A SECOND LANGUAGE Jamie Sobrato
Lust in Translation, Bk. 1

Ariel Turner's sexual tour of Europe has landed her in Italy seeking the perfect Italian lover. But despite the friendliness of the locals, she's not having much luck. Until the day the very hot Marc Sorrella sits beside her. Could it be she's found the ideal candidate?

#317 THE HAUNTING Hope Tarr
Extreme

History professor Maggie Holliday's new antebellum home has everything she's ever wanted—including the ghost of Captain Ethan O'Malley, a Union soldier who insists Maggie's the reincarnation of his lost love. And after one incredibly sexual night in his arms, she's inclined to believe him....

#318 AT HIS FINGERTIPS Dawn Atkins
Doing it...Better! Bk. 3

When a fortune-teller predicts the return of a man from her past, Esmeralda McElroy doesn't expect Mitch Margolin. The sexy sizzle is still between them, but he's a lot more cautious than she remembers. Does this mean she'll have to seduce him to his senses?

#319 BAD BEHAVIOR Kristin Hardy
Sex & the Supper Club II, Bk. 3

Dominick Gordon can't believe it. He thinks his eyes are playing tricks on him when he spots the older, but no less beautiful, Delaney Phillips—it's been almost twenty years since they dated as teenagers. Still, Dom's immediate feelings show he's all man, and Delaney's all woman....

#320 ALL OVER YOU Sarah Mayberry
Secret Lives of Daytime Divas, Bk. 2

The last thing scriptwriter Grace Wellington wants is for the man of her fantasies to step into her life. But Mac Harrison, in his full, gorgeous glory, has done exactly that. Worse, they're now working together. That is, if Grace can keep her hands to herself!

HBCNM0307